4TH
&
GOAL.
publishing

thoughts for Thots

BRODY MCVITTIE

Introduction.

Look,

It's not to say that Billy isn't a motherfucker—it's not to say that Malik is an angel. DeShawn shouldn't be trusted either; Big Tim really isn't all that big, despite the clever and original handle on social.

Speaking of, there are plenty of socially inept, morally bankrupt sociopaths on the male spectrum; it stands to reason that there's the odd deviant amongst the non-binary and LGBTQ2+ communities also.

This isn't the book for them.

*The Meathead Manifesto, my masterpiece from the early aughts, detailed the shortcomings of gym-culture bros and suitably skewered the emotionally-stunted-ness of The Fuckboi Pandemic. Go read that to get your hate on for the misgivings of the testosterone-surplus crowd.

This is aimed at That Hoe Over There; the THOT community more concerned with social media clout than advancing their standing through more conventional (read: antiquated) means.

This is for the subsect of society that embraces thong-bikini selfies indoors, the behind-a-paywall-for-titties earners that are building a brand on the strength of symmetrical nipples.

This is a love-letter/helpful handbook for the twerkers; the OnlyFans (-and-a-lot-of-them) collective more interested in that paid vacation, the hell with how they earn it.

God Bless Them All.

This, presented humbly and after significant scientific research, is:

Thoughts for Thots.

BOOK ONE

You

thoughts for Thots.

CHAPTER ONE

Your new man is better looking.

*and other lies you tell yourself.

*and me.

*and anyone who will listen.

thoughts for Thots.

He broke up with you.

Maybe he told you why maybe he didn't.

Maybe he rationalized it with ruminations on geography or a change in matters of import between the two of you.

He might have cried a little. Or a lot. (Really, either is a sign you shouldn't be with his ass, but that's a subject for another time.)

He might have lied when he said he would keep in touch; he might have lied when he said it wasn't you.

It was you.

He's tired of the pussy, or maybe the side pussy did enough behind the scenes and under the motel sheets to snuggle up to that main-girl slot.

Either-and-any-way-you-slice-it, he's over you and onto the next.

*You have to understand, this is Chapter One because it is the catalyst for the birth of the THOT; the embryo from which a morally carefree, disdainfully liberated butterfly will emerge, beating her proverbial wings (ass cheeks) to the tune of whatever is top of the Hip-Hop charts by the time this book comes out, some six months before it is yanked off the shelves for offending some SJW cucks.

But back to you.

You're newly re-invented, scantily-clad, and determined to find the next man.

You do, maybe at the behest of a buddy who—tired of your misery-filled text messages—tells you that Johnny has been into you for years and that he's a perfect guy.

And that it's okay that he still lives with his parents because he's *got plans*.

You go on a first date, somewhere unpretentious and cozy, somewhere like *Jack Astor's* or *Crabby Joe's* or insert-platonic-not-at-all-imaginative-or-remotely-romantic restaurant.

Something Johnny suggested because Johnny's got no creative impulses whatsoever.

(Which you tell yourself is refreshing because the guy who just dumped your ass was a little *too* creative—and your poor little anus is still not the same.)

So you're sitting across—or, if you're particularly tasteless—beside Johnny in some booth in some shitty restaurant, and you're subconsciously telling yourself that his glaring inadequacies are cute because Johnny is earnest and smiling hard. And you can tell he'd really like to fuck you.

*Again, refreshing.

So, somewhere between that third bite of cheesy bread and cocktail-too-many, you decide to give good old Johnny a shot. Because it can't be worse for you than that last asshole was.

...

Maybe you get through that first night—and, if you're really lucky—that first-time uncomfortable fumbling you call sex—before the comparisons come creeping in.

Sometime between meeting his parents and kind-of moving him into your modest one-bedroom studio apartment, however, they inevitably do.

First, and probably most importantly: he's just not as good-looking.

Which is troubling for a number of reasons—paramount among them, the fact that you tell yourself that he *is*.

Now, your delusion—while cute—is also somewhat understandable. You did just get out of what you're now calling a horribly toxic relationship; you almost can't be blamed if your overactive little endorphins have tricked you into believing the gap-toothed mouth-breather you're now tragically cohabitating with can hold a candle to your former lover.

Sure, your little asshole is somewhat less sore, and sure, having someone unabashedly put you first is *just that*—a first—but at some point, you kind of owe it to yourself to be honest.

Johnny is a lot of things; dedicated cunnilingist, devoted cuddler, emasculated shotgun-seat rider. He loves long walks in the park—maybe even inline skating—and he cooks a mean grilled cheese sandwich.

But he's got two abs where your ex had at least six, and his tongue game is compensating for inches somewhat less than astonishing, and his lazy eye isn't quite as rogue-ish as the one before.

His hair is kind of fucky, and that's to say nothing of the back-pussy tufting up from the rim of his undersized pink short-shorts.

The warning signs you ignored when his closet space dominated yours (to say nothing of his proclivity for pastels) were glaring, sure, but the reassurances of friends relieved not to have to deal with your whiny bullshit have blinded you to the fact he's a little bit lacking.

The collective

Girl, he's so cute

You're so lucky

I swear all of my friends are in LOVE with him

Ugh, I'm so jealous

Bitch, you're the hottest thing on the market

Johnny won't shut up about you

In five years, he's gonna be the top associate at (insert pyramid scheme)

He had a real shot at the (semi) pros before he blew his meniscus in Grade 10

I'm in love LOVE with the way he looks at you

He's. So. Trendy.

I love you too so much I could DIE

insights from equally-unhappy acquaintances have fooled you into believing he's an equal match.

…

Your parents only like him because he's stable, but stable is about as exotic as those fucking grilled cheese sandwiches he keeps culinary delighting you with.

He's into making love and talking about feelings, and you tell your only-slightly-less-annoyed-than-they-were-when-you-were-crying friends that you can see yourself having his testosterone-lacking offspring.

You're under the illusion that you're happy—happier than you were when Wednesdays were for light sodomy and heartbreak, and so you're glowing, but only in that toxic-waste-radioactive way.

CHAPTER TWO

You're doing just fine.

thoughts for Thots.

You're not.

And that's okay—you just spent one, or two, or three years of your life believing that Esteban (Steve) was the one; that the townhouse you shared would eventually see the office downstairs converted to an infant room.

You were happy, blissfully unaware of the trouble brewing behind Esteban (Steve's) passcode-protected home screen. See, Esteban (Steve) loves strange pussy— and for one or two or three years, he was at the very least entertaining/exploring the idea of cheating on your ass.

Of course, he eventually did/" didn't;" either way, the townhouse you were hoping would eventually house your children now houses his younger/firmer-than-you sidepiece. (I guess, in a way, maybe Esteban/(Steve's) place ended up with children after all.)

Regardless, you're angry and understandably and jaded and justifiably, and you're practically living at your friend Tiffany's place. It's cramped, and you call it cozy, and her dog is shedding/dying on her futon/your bed, but you're *fine*.

Right?

You're doing-fine/revenge plan begins to take shape; a large portion of it involves revealing your shape on social in order to attract a version of Esteban/(Steve) that won't hurt you.

(*This version does not exist, but bless your heart for trying.)

Your inner THOT is beginning to emerge; that first ass pic is getting the kinds of likes you'd previously imagined only existed for B-grade Influencers. This is inspiring— the attention is overwhelming, and the DM's are equally uplifting/horrifying.

(*More of that in Chapter Three, 'Darkness in the DM's.')

You're out on dates with a series of increasingly questionable men; men like Trevor the Future Capitalist, men like Mike the career student. Sure, our boy Johnny from Chapter One is *going* places—but living at home unseasonably into his twenties requires a level of oversight you really should reconsider.

So you're three or four weeks removed from having your world upended, but you've stopped shaking in the shower, and you've rediscovered the thunder/power in your ass cheeks, and you've bonded with your old friend Tiffany and, even though you're violently allergic to her dog, you're sleeping just a little more soundly.

You're choosing/dating men like Trevor the Future Capitalist and Mike the career student and Johnny the basement dweller, and you're taking advantage of the current social climate's appreciation of sideboob. There's an electricity to your newfound freedom, and you suppose it doesn't matter that said freedom was forced upon you.

Pivoting is a buzzword for spiraling, and taking the time to process the significant shift in your life doesn't trend with how an empowered, liberated woman operates.

So it's onwards and to the next set of circumstances that may (or, to be fair, may not) yield similar/devastating results. You're blissfully unaware that Esteban/(Steve) has just become The Motherfucker Who Caused All This (TMFWCAT) and that Johnny is just the first of the rest to hurt you since.

CHAPTER THREE

Darkness in the DM's.

thoughts for Thots.

Mike just wants to see your titties.

Ricardo-Gustavo (if that's even his real name) talks about his feelings more than your girlfriends.

Nate is the kind of boring even you, in these volatile, desperate times, can't entertain; Troy just wants to see your titties.

Whoever is lurking behind the handle of @HotBoi69 is a certified sex pervert; @bigmeech uses more emojis than your girlfriends.

You were having innocent, platonic conversations with work associates and couples-vacation post admirers; occasionally, an ex would reach out with a thinly-veiled "mom asked about you the other day" attempt at stirring things back up.

And then you posted that ass pic.

...

Let's back up a little.

It's not like the ass pic, strategically lit in your bedroom and filtered at least as aggressively as your limited photoshopping skills allowed came out of nowhere. No, first you had to emerge from what is now, in hindsight, an incredibly toxic relationship with a man who just didn't *get* you. You had to reflect this status on Instagram, first with a strategically vague series of story posts quoting other woke feminists preaching the virtue of thriving independently.

You followed that up with the removal of any evidence of that horribly toxic relationship from your timeline, even though it kind of broke your heart to take down those bikini pics from that one time the useless fucker took you to some three-star resort in Mexico.

Next came the public-status enabling on Insta, followed directly by the one-two punch of some sassy bio tagline and the reactivation of Snapchat. You rationalized this, of course, by claiming it to be your preferred method of communicating to commiserating singles and moved-on college associates.

The whole Tinder thing, though?

Even you had trouble rationalizing that one. Still, there was wine involved, the way wine kind of rides shotgun on all of your decision making now—no doubt there was a glass of it resting on the counter you cropped out in the first of what will be a glorious descent into increasingly-suggestive thirst traps.

Which brings me back to the ass pic and the deluge of welcomed/completely unwelcomed attention it has created for you.

Circling back on some of the more adventurous messages you've received, instantly and at a subsequently steady pace since the wine suggested you post:

Shane, it turns out, appreciates the ass but is really interested in your toes.

Margaret, surprisingly, is a fan/new follower from Australia. You quickly break off into tangent conversations on topics ranging from *FashionNova* dresses to nail polish hacks to environmentalism; eventually, though, she asks to see your titties.

Similarly, @brent84, Dennis, and someone who may very well turn out to be your sixth-grade English teacher are desperately campaigning for the creation of your *OnlyFans.*

(*Best believe we will dive into that topic later.)

You have at least three invitations to become Brand Ambassador to some shady clothing companies with sub-one-thousand followers. You're so flattered at this you ignore the little wrinkle that you'd have to pay them for the opportunity to post wearing their respective brands.

The coup-de-grace, however, doesn't come until you've gained scores of new followers and been reposted on @bikinihoes or @tushymonsters or some equally offensive (--but kind of cool, right?) hack accounts.

No, the real darkness in your DMs creeps in sometime around 2:30 am your time, when the wine has pacified the tumultuous reminiscing that makes up the first two hours of attempted sleep.

It hits you when you open your social channels the next morning, just after you put on the hot secretary glasses you're thinking of wearing while chewing a pencil in your next post.

That's the moment you discover some Saudi Prince from some territory you've never heard of wants to fly you out on his private jet for an all-expenses-paid vacation.

It's probably 9:34 am, and—if I had to point to a single, cataclysmic moment when your inner THOT was violently unleashed—it's right now, just after double-tapping *love* on his written proposition.

CHAPTER FOUR

What your search history says about you.

thoughts for Thots.

Nothing good.

Here's some hotness, pulled directly from the nonsensical should-just-be-inner-monologuing you're feverishly typing into the poor Google Search engine:

-what Plastic Surgery will make me hotter

-floating ribs removal cost

-floating ribs removal recovery time

-floating ribs surgery videos (*this required a quick drive to YouTube, which you regretted violently some twenty-two minutes and three and a half videos later.)

-Kylie Jenner lip serum

-Kylie Jenner lip injections

-Kylie Jenner lip injections doctor

-lip injection clinics near me

-breast enhancement surgery cost (duh)

-Brazilian Butt Lift cost

-boobs & ass surgery discount

-something called 'CoolSculpting' followed by dozens of trips to YouTube and Instagram to watch similarly enhanced Influencers pretend that they developed *that* ass by doing band-assisted lateral lunges.

None of this is overly concerning; best believe those of us on the Fuckboi side are asking equally ridiculous information of our overworked search engines also. And, alarmingly, the inquires lead to many of the same websites. The concern begins to climb, however, when that 30-day free trial to 'seekingromanticencounters.com' or 'sugarbabiesunleashed.com' or 'camsluts.org' begin to see your pretty little fingers click *Register*.

Suddenly it's less

-best self-tanner

-self-tanner mitt re-order

-smallest bikini possible shop

and more

-how much do cam girls make

and

-do Sugar Daddies expect sex on the first date

and

a whole hell of a lot of what might be a tad unhealthy research.

Still, you're just at the research stage, and 'casualhookups.net' is just another social networking channel/opportunity. So there's no harm in cheeky pseudonyms and profile pics that are indistinguishable to anyone aside from the increasingly larger subsect of your following who might recognize that beauty mark on your favorite ass cheek.

CHAPTER FIVE

He's just not that into you.

(Either.)

thoughts for Thots.

Johnny's been a bad boy.

Which tracks—and this isn't an observation regarding your taste in men—more of an affectation that you're *into* men. Not to say that there aren't any good ones out there; to be fair, you wouldn't have any interest in reading this book if you were drawn to them. You're not, and that's okay.

I'm not a good man either, which is why I'm able to write a book like this. It stands to reason that I don't surround myself with good men—or good women—hence my invaluable insight into your current predicament.

We're back to Johnny, your last/best chance at remaining the not-jaded-not-THOT you were before the asshole before Johnny left your ass. You may be unconsciously blissful, here in the beginning stages of what you're hoping will be the relationship that works. You're maybe teaching him to cook something other than fucking grilled cheese; Johnny might even be learning, pretending to be interested in anything other than the ass that's potentially about to make you D-level famous.

What you don't realize? Every time Johnny takes his phone and excuses himself to the bathroom, he's at the very least staring at D-level famous girls he'd love to fuck, also. Which is totally cool because his social feeds are so inundated with girls with asses at least as fat as yours that he's low-key desensitized to them.

At some point, it all just becomes museum-style displays of artificially enhanced anatomy.

Artificially enhanced anatomy he'd love to penetrate, but hey, he'd love not to have to cook his dinner, either.

No, the danger lurks in the DMs; in his case, the DMs he's sending to co-workers and ex girls just like you and—if he's a real scumbag—the girls with asses at least as fat as yours. The girls he's 'just friends' with.

Now, if Johnny is any kind of good-looking (and, as established in our very first chapter, he's not as good-looking as the guy who dumped your ass) then you had better believe girls with asses at least as fat as yours are sliding into his DMs too.

This is actually the one area where a not-that-good-looking rebound man can be of benefit. You've got a fighting chance that the hoes clamoring for your main piece status aren't superior in the looks/relatively fatter ass department.

So while you're in the kitchen stirring applesauce or whatever the fuck gets stirred in kitchens, be mindful of Johnny's semi-frequent bathroom excursions and what they could mean for your collective future.

. . .

There's this girl at Johnny's work.

If she comes up in conversation over dinner, or anytime at all, then if he's not fucking her, you had better believe he's actively trying to. Men are simple/single-minded, especially when it comes to the consumption of food or women. If Becky's name is brought up over applesauce, recognize you might have to cut a bitch.

You see, Becky is a problem the way they're all potentially a problem; the way you're likely part of the problem, too, sensitive to losing the next one you care about over the same shit you likely lost the last one to. The predicament is cooking like applesauce on that stovetop (again, assuming applesauce cooks), and you're left with only a couple of uncomfortable options.

You could confront him about the bitches like Becky; the bitches who come up in conversation a lot more than your maybe-overly-sensitive-but-woke-regardless ass is comfortable with. Of course, this approach could lend itself to rebuttals with words like 'crazy' in them, or vague deflections, or the classic "what about that guy from work you talk about" question that, depending on the level of your descent into THOTness, you may not be comfortable answering.

You could take the passive-aggressive approach, bringing up oh-so-subtle observations like "you know who has exquisite style? Becky." Gauge his responses, cataloging them over time and in one of those manila file folders in the corner of your mind reserved for schemes comma revenge. You could collect data on her socials; is Johnny spending time in her comments, or is she invading the sanctity of his profile, leaving likes where they shouldn't be.

You could go super cerebral and strike up a 'friendship' with the bitch; spending an afternoon together away from Johnny will undoubtedly have his palms sweating if he's established an emotional connection with her based on her having a vagina that isn't yours.

You could take it one step further and hook her up with one of your male 'friends' (read: the guys who talk to you in hopes of fucking you on the side…note their dramatic increase in numbers since that first ass pic went live.) This will elicit an exceedingly jealous response from Johnny should his plans to groom Becky be trifled with.

You could get out while the getting's good; cut your losses for the past three or six or nine months and finally recognize that a) Johnny was a rebound and b) he wasn't the good guy the wine told you he was on that first, semi-desperate date and c) maybe you really should spend some time alone the way no one except your cousin Debbie suggested. Of course, you ignored her because Debbie is a cunt. But that doesn't mean she was wrong.

(*Quick aside- I recognize your Mom likes Johnny, but you need to understand that bitch's opinion doesn't count. She's terrified you'll end up alone.)

Of course, you could wait until you catch the passcode on his phone during one of your action-movie (his choice, naturally) showcase snuggles. Next Friday, sometime between picking his drunk ass up from the bar and holding his hair back while he vomits in the toilet of your cozy one-bedroom studio apartment, you'll see a notification notice pop up on his phone, and you'll naturally wonder who could be so concerned at 3:24 am. You'll input the 1234 or TITS code and notice that Becky has sent six messages since he left the bar and got into your car. (This is some thirteen messages after texting him yourself to tell him you've been outside waiting for his drunk ass for the better part of the half-hour you now recognize you wasted while he was in said bar making out with Becky.)

Which hurts, and not just because his friends who were supposed to be your friends too were in the bar witnessing these no-longer-alleged-but-really-confirmed infidelities, confirmed as of text two on the phone you're spying on, text two

I miss you already

sometime after text one

That was fun devil-emoji-water-splash-emoji

but before

text four,

which isn't even a text but a picture of Becky's not even as good as your titties,

just above text six

wish you were here.

CHAPTER SIX

He was never really there.

thoughts for Thots.

Sometime between leaving Johnny's worthless ass and establishing your OnlyFans account, you're going to reach out to TMFWCAT (The Mother Fucker Who Caused All This), and you're going to want answers.

Answers about "how could he" and "were any of the insert-number-of-years-wasted/together real" and "do you ever miss us" and all of the other bullshit you waste nights imagining answers to.

You'll message him, or call him, or suggest you meet for coffee, depending on the severity of the desperation eating away at your rapidly already-eaten soul. (*Or maybe you won't message him at all, already well on your way to embracing your inner THOT and with no time to reminisce on his fool ass. In this case, congratulations, it's on to Chapter Seven.)

However, for those of you still here, it's important to note that you'll be approaching said potential reunion coffee with slightly varying motivations.

You'll be showing up to the agreed-upon coffeeshop looking as desirable as you're able to, hoping to elicit some pang of pain at his sure-to-happen realization that leaving your ass was a terrible mistake. You're hoping to gain valuable insight into the machinations of a scumbag's mind. You're searching for validation that you've been better off on your own. You're seeking confirmation to your girlfriend's theory that you were too good for him all along and that it simply took (insert number of years wasted/together) for you to finally realize it. You're hoping to establish some common ground, strike up an understanding that could potentially blossom into a friendship, or—in the most extreme case—help him finally see that he is still madly in love with you. And then maybe begin a months-long campaign of expensive gift receiving and exotic date attempts before finally allowing his sufficiently-groveled ass back into your cozy one-bedroom apartment bed.

He's looking to fuck you in the ass in the backseat of the car he parked out back, two parking spaces from the dumpster.

So romance is suggestive—either way, you agree on the meeting for various reasons and go about preparations for said coffee.

...

He looks good, sitting at the coffee shop table on the patio just around the corner from your cozy one-bedroom apartment. This is annoying for at least two reasons—one, you had strategically suggested this particular coffeeshop precisely due to said proximity, hoping to beat him here and make him awkwardly navigate the crowded space while you sit all resplendent and shit, and two, the motherfucker was never on time for anything, ever, the entirety of your three years together.

He's smiling that cocksure, Cheshire smile—the one you

only admit to yourself you used to love when you're a bottle of wine and three pills deep. You're suddenly thinking about wine, goddammit, and wishing you had suggested some bar instead, arriving here *second* and already failed in the first of your silly little schemes to elicit a jealous response.

Regardless, you're newly single and powerful and the type of enlightened woman who can take on the world. And so you fake your friendliest smile, and you sway your sufficiently ample hips, and you sit your just-fat-enough ass in the chair the bastard couldn't be bothered to stand up and pull out for you.

The conversation begins pleasantly, the pre-requisite volley of niceties lobbed back and forth while you patiently wait for the suddenly all-too-absent waiter to bring his ass over. You can't tell whether or not you appreciate the up/down his eyes are continuously doing as you describe your cozy one-bedroom apartment; on the one hand, you maybe enjoy the non-verbal affirmation that you really do look great in the dress you fasted all day to fit in. On the other hand, his sudden interest in the breasts he took for granted for years is bubbling-just-under-the-surface revolting.

So you're sitting there, patio on the coffeeshop you suggested, and you're waiting for the waiter, and you're wishing this was one of those trendy wine/coffee shops, and you're wondering if this was a good idea after all.

It's not, but you're committed, and you tell yourself that maybe you needed this to cement the fact that the answers you were looking for might not exist, let alone manifest themselves throughout this slightly-more-uncomfortable-than-you-imagined conversation.

You break eye contact with his frustratingly still beautiful ones, and you scan relentlessly for the waiter, and you commit to the coffee, and the mistakes you're suddenly sure are to follow.

CHAPTER SEVEN

Sad puss.

thoughts for Thots.

You fucked him.

Things were going so well; you'd realized that Johnny wasn't any good for you. You'd found both a sense of liberation and newfound popularity with just one empowering ass shot—you'd just recognized the value of some much needed time alone...

...and then you went for coffee.

Which fucked absolutely everything up because you're walking shamefully from TMFWCAT's (The Mother Fucker Who Caused All This) townhouse that used to be *your* townhouse and, before leaving, you had nostalgic nausea regarding just how much you maybe actually missed it. You're thinking about how annoyingly pleasant the fucking itself was, maybe confusing a comfortability and a carnal knowledge of how to get you off with the passion you've been missing in sexual encounters since. Still, there was coldness and a decided lack of coffee in the morning, and he got dressed for work with a finality that suggested this was more a hole to fill literally than metaphorically.

He offered to pay for the Uber you turned down on principle, collecting your panties if not your pride and assuring him you'll both walk and be fine. You figure the cold of pavement has to be at least a little warmer than the embrace he kinda gave you before closing the door, literally and also maybe metaphorically.

You weren't sure what you had wanted, aside from making him feel as though leaving you was a horrible mistake, but you're reasonably sure that a) this wasn't it, and b) the horrible mistake is all yours. You've given him the power back, allowed him to degrade you to coffeeshop hookup status, and emerged--from the coffeeshop date you weren't sure about—sure about having blown it.

And him, which contributes to the low you feel as you walk across town to the cozy one-bedroom apartment you moved back into full-time when you couldn't stand crashing at Tiffany's anymore. The apartment unmercifully across the street from the coffee shop your night should have ended at. You feel a little dirty, and you feel a little confused, and you feel a little too sober, turning the key and allowing the store décor and distinct lack of space to remind you of what else you'd lost when TMFWCAT decided you were less *forever* and more *every-now-and-then.*

You slump onto the bed that doubles as your couch, and maybe you take a minute before you pick up your phone/laptop, and you begin to craft a thorough revenge plan. And the revenge isn't against him, necessarily—no, it's more of a fuck-everyone who would dare fuck with you by fucking with them thoroughly-and first-kinda plan.

It begins, this plan, by taking off the majority of your clothes and rolling around suggestively on your bed/couch and taking the rest of the sixty-two-before-it's-right-semi-nudes that you'll photoshop and filter and, eventually, (exhausted) post.

The sadness of your coffeeshop quest for absolution/descent into degradation only has you feeling down for the minutes it takes until the likes, and the comments, and the DMs pull you in a distinctly more positive headspace.

Suddenly you're navigating a torrent of not-at-all arousing dick pics and lewd requests to drink your bath water or massage your feet/suck your toes or chain you up to some bed/couch that isn't your own; you're filtering through them, and you're equal parts flattered and emboldened and ready to swear off men forever when someone you knew two jobs and four hairstyles ago messages you with an utterly unique

"Hey."

CHAPTER EIGHT

"He's different".

thoughts for Thots.

You don't need a man to validate you.

You don't need to be in a relationship—or some semblance of—to feel beautiful or wanted or complete. You like men—and dating them—because you're horny and you're hot and *fuck them* anyways.

You're learning to play the game, toying with them the way a cat sadistically toys with a mouse, pulling off non-vital limbs, and gnawing at rubbery parts before sinking a projectile paw through the brainstem. And yes, it might be reaching, as analogies go, but if the boys are going to be vulgar and omnipresent and easily-digestible, you can't be blamed for partaking.

Brad is really close to paying your rent in exchange for semi-nudes (and this is before you really go down the Sugar Baby road). Chris T swears he'll fly you out to Vegas. You can practically smell Dimitri's cologne through the phone; his misplaced confidence will require a significant dismantling. Angus swears it's his real name; @Bearrcubb42 might be a little confused.

You're having fun with all of them, appreciating their collective reverence and rewarding them—to varying degrees—with the kind of (disappearing, naturally) pics that have gained you close to twenty-five thousand new followers.

Every now and then, between basking in adulation and coming up with increasingly aggressive/suggestive thirst traps, you receive a new message or series-of from that guy who knew you two jobs and four hairstyles ago.

Which is worth noting—if and for no other reason because his messages aren't requests to mail him your panties or spend time in his basement or move your big toe semi-permanently into his anus. His messages are concerns (and genuine ones) regarding the status of your day. His conversations—when you're brave enough to engage them—involve the socio-political system and your favorite movies and talks about just what your life has been like for the past two jobs and four hairstyles. He debates art and Katy Perry's place in pop culture; he tells you he's taken up golf and that he's got a place outside the city.

It all sounds lovely, and it's refreshing, and you remember him being handsome way back when which is probably paramount among reasons he and his conversations are generally ignored.

Ignored in favor of Lothar's insistence you send him daily nudes and ignored because Travis has a rose tattooed on the side of his face (and this makes his complete lack of responsibility desirable) and ignored because you'd rather engage @chloeluxx and her request to film a bubble bath together next weekend.

CHAPTER NINE

Fuckbois suck, too.

thoughts for Thots.

They really do.

They're handsome, which is how they get away with it, and horny, which is why they can't go five DMs past

Hello

or

You up

without sending you a picture of their cocks.

They're manipulative somehow; able to coerce the sweetest, most pure among you to show far more than you should, six messages into an initial conversation.

Good thing you're no longer the sweetest or most pure.

So you fuck with them, these Fuckbois, accepting their follow requests and faking interest in their profiles. You engage in polite conversation occasionally and always when the conversation *isn't*. You pretend that what they have to say is interesting; you wait behind a glass of wine and a cynical smile for the inevitable dick pic to arrive. You're kind in your assessment, cruel when their aggression becomes unwelcome.

The truth is that there is no such thing as a good dick pic. It's always ruined by lighting or angle or facial expression or anything—and this is before acknowledging the penis itself doesn't lend to a photogenic presentation.

You humor them because they're pathetic, more often than not, so far out of your newly-elevated league that their collective delusions are fodder for the confidence growing with each welcome submission. Bent cocks, uncircumcised hairy cocks, more than you'd even imagined stumpy cocks. Skinny cocks, circumcised hairy cocks, left-leaning-doesn't-even-make-sense cocks. Micrococks. Cocks of every color. They're as varied as the demographic sometimes kind enough to send messages alongside them; messages with words like

beautiful

and

gorgeous

in them; messages that can't help but make you feel better about the situation you've found yourself in.

...

Until you decide, you might maybe want something more.

After a time, it grows tiring, these cyber interactions with undeserving Fuckbois, their superficial platitudes doing little to satiate that part of you craving human interaction.

You know it's likely going to end in disaster, but you decide it might be time to venture out into the world and meet them.

Date #1: Rad Chad.

Rad Chad is a TikTok personality, which is to say he has none. He talks in fifteen-second bursts, here on the patio of the pub you reluctantly agreed to meet him at. It's dimly-lit, which is a miracle because every single time the light catches the reflection of a diamond stud in his ear, you're blinded (like now), and for the next fifteen-second outburst he's in the middle of. This one is about his watch, which he's making sound nice, but it looks gaudy and ridiculous and entirely unnecessary.

Kind of like Rad Chad, and kind of like this date.

Still, you post about it, and you gain a legion of new and what must be avid TikTok fans.

Which makes considering the blowjob he begs for in the parking lot after the hug goodbye worth it, but—unfortunately for Rad Chad—he's just not that attractive, and so you pass.

Date #2: Varsity Zach.

Varsity Zach is Zach with an 'h,' which was almost enough to make this date never happen. Still, Varsity Zach is hot, and he's got abs where his belly button (and below that too) should be, and he wasn't afraid to show them to you two messages before the message within which he suggested *this* date, so you agreed because why the hell not. You make out with Varsity Zach, here on date one, because he's hot and you're drunk, and you're drinking, still, and because he doesn't mind that halfway through your first kiss, you spilled half your vodka soda on his better-off-wet t-shirt. Which you tell him to take off, but Varsity Zach is showing the kind of restraint you're admittedly not used to from a Fuckboi. This behavior is refreshing and confusing and remains that way until halfway through the night, some of Varsity Zach's buddies show up, and the attention that should be solely on you turns to just about everyone but.

You leave Date #2 a little disappointed. You notice, in leaving, that—judging by the amount of time Varsity Zach is spending with Varsity Shawn—you might not be the *only* confused single tonight.

Date #3: Jim (no last name given)

Jim likes to fuck.

You know this because he tells you.

Right away.

Which is bold, as conversation ice-breakers go, but you're once again reminded that you're on a date with a Fuckboi.

So you take it on the chin (no doubt the way he wants you to), and you remind yourself that you're here to take advantage of the attention and the adulation and the lust. Jim has brought you here, to what has to be one of the most expensive restaurants in the city, and he's treating you to champagne and caviar, which you've never tasted but have to admit is quite delicious. And so Jim and his forthcoming expansions on tonight's dinner conversation are to be semi-tolerated. You're amused, and you might even be somewhat interested, finding his confidence/arrogance amusing, until he takes a deep dive into topics like restrained sodomy and mild electrocution.

So Jim blows it (no doubt the way he wishes you would) well before whatever expensive dessert he's ordered arrives. You excuse yourself to the washroom and sneak out the back, confident that you've, at the very least, saved yourself a week of uncomfortable sitting.

Date #4: Tony! Tony! Tony!

Tony gets it, meaning he gives it to you, over and over.

You figure why not; you're hot and single, and he's hot, and there is absolutely nothing wrong with getting what you want (*off) and then kicking Tony out of your cozy little one-bedroom apartment and telling yourself you'll do your best never to call him again.

Date #5: Cory the maybe-future Doctor

Cory might be a doctor one day; that is, if he can successfully graduate med school. Which makes his Fuckboi escapades somewhat impressive—that he can maintain decent study habits while sexualizing every woman he meets online. It's a juggling act, you imagine—which makes Cory either interesting, as Fuckbois go, or a sociopath, or both. He's an irregularity somewhat—you're used to a certain level of not-having-their-shit-together from the men you're meeting online, which hasn't stopped you from meeting/taking what you want from them, using them for dates and dinners, and getting off the way you deserve to. Admittedly, Cory-the-maybe-future-Doctor is refreshing—an example of how the Fuckboi can come in any shape or size or socio-economic background. His motives aren't nearly as unique as his aspirations—thirteen messages in he's asking to see your tits—but after a deluge of mouth-breathing basement dwellers, Cory-the-maybe-future-Doctor is a nice change of pace.

Which earns him dates comma many, dates like this one, mini-putt with Cory-the maybe-future-Doctor. He talks a big game, pulling up to the mini-putt place in his not-sure-what-model-but-expensive Audi and letting you spill Starbucks on the leather and not giving you hell for it.

He plays a mean game, too, draining putts like a motherfucker and making a series of increasingly sexual bets for every hole filled (for every hole filled.)

You play along because you want to and because it's the kind of fun he is, and it's the kind of fun you've been missing. By the hole with the giant spinning windmill, you're letting him insert his tongue down your throat, and you're letting him insert his fingers somewhere underneath your too-short-for-mini-putt skirt.

You're learning that there are levels to this Fuckboi shit, and your previously all-encompassing determinations as to the viability of the species are melting faster than the ice cream he buys you after the game.

CHAPTER TEN

Steady creepin'

thoughts for Thots.

It doesn't last.

Which comes as no surprise, and you knew it, your experiences with TMFWCAT and Johnny and—going back—maybe your father and maybe that camp counselor at that bible retreat—preparing you for the eventual fuckery that comes with dating a Fuckboi.

Which Cory is, maybe-future-Doctor or not.

It starts slow, his descent into mistreating you—he blows off a date two dates after mini-putt/licking ice cream off of your asshole, claiming Med School *something* has him pinned down for the foreseeable future.

Which is entirely understandable and by no means a big deal—until the next three dates are planned and similarly not executed, for the same reasons.

You're trying to be understanding, thinking back on your own educational experiences, and vaguely remembering specific periods of overwhelming panic—but you're subconsciously mapping the frequency of successfully executed dates *pre*-sex and noticing a distinct difference in the ratio *post*-anal.

That is, until Saturday night—the same Saturday night he broke plans with you to go out drinking with his buddies. Which you, somewhat strangely (being the new/hopefully sole object of his affections), weren't invited to.

Until 1:30 am.

Of course, you're still not invited, rumbling from semi-peaceful slumber to receive a string of poorly executed text messages.

He's invited—or so he hopes—to share the bed he's so mercilessly risen you from, tasking you with meeting his drunk ass in the lobby so you can help him stumble from the Uber he falls out of.

It's a far cry from the not-sure-what-model-but-expensive Audi, but you're clinging to hope this is all in your head the way you're clinging to Cory-the-maybe-future-Doctor in the elevator you hold him up in. All the way to the top, floor thirteen a rarity—but, just your luck—alive and well in the building you were forced to find all those months ago, dumped and kicked out and reflecting, watching yourself hold some other asshole up in the reflection of the elevator mirror, waiting to hit that peak.

He's peeking, Cory-the-maybe-future-Doctor, and down your admittedly-revealing-because-it's-what-you-sleep-in top, all of his roguish charm evaporated, leaving a fumbling, child-like mess for you to clean as you attempt to enter your cozy little one-bedroom apartment.

Holding his hair back while he vomits is inducing flashbacks of holding Johnny's hair back while he vomits, and you're staring at the pattern on the tile of the bathroom, and you're starting to see a pattern. The boys you're drawn to are the boys who prefer their Fridays and Saturdays out at bars, and now Cory-the-maybe-future

-Doctor is turning out like Johnny the-last-guy-you-were-foolish-enough-to-take-a-chance-on and the last guy you told yourself you'd fall for.

So you don't fall for it, leaving Cory's unprotected phone on the nightstand and choosing not to investigate the Fuckboi machinations dwelling just beneath that lock screen; opting instead to put Cory-the-maybe-future-Doctor to bed with the delicate touch of a motherfucking Neurosurgeon, curling away from his still-heaving body and entering the deepest sleep possible, given the neuroses crashing like waves on your subconscious.

CHAPTER ELEVEN

Post notifications ?

(you're not over it.)

thoughts for Thots.

You're really not.

And it's not okay.

He posts—TMFWCAT (The Mother Fucker Who Caused All This) about the girls he's out on dates with, the girls that aren't you, pretty and perky, and always seeming really pleased to be in whatever circumstance the picture in the post you're creeping on called for.

You know this because you kept your Post Notifications on, content to torture yourself every single time he decides to subliminally reach out from across the internet and ruin your day/week/month/year/life. He does—post—often, pictures of sunset beaches and cobblestone street walks somewhere far and riding on some of those oversized Ferris wheels.

He's looking appropriately magnificent in all of them; his hair is trendier, somehow, and the stubble on the chin you used to love has grown into a resplendent beard. There's a little grey in it—you know this because you zoom in on his pics, and you analyze them a hell of a lot more than you should. It makes you feel a little more than it should, too; every time the banner on your phone appears signaling he's made a new post, you're quick to scrutinize every detail of it. You tell yourself it's understandable; a little detective work completely normal in the face of having your life upended without concrete reasons why. As more time passes—and with more and more men between you and the you you used to be—you're running out of rationalizations.

You're making them anyways, telling yourself that by gathering intel, you're gathering insight into his sociopathic psyche—knowing the next post or the next post will finally unlock some dormant feeling as to why you're so much better off without him.

It hasn't happened yet—but, to be fair, it's only been a number of months and dozens of posts—but you tell yourself you're sure it will. And so you investigate/scrutinize—fast—jumping over the notifications as soon as they appear; appear like they do right now, in the middle of some date barely worth mentioning.

It comes in hot, today's banner alert, screaming at you from the phone you've rested on the table between you and Todd, tonight's date being one you shouldn't have agreed to based on his name alone. You reach for it before he mouth-breathes whatever bullshit he was midway through getting to before the alert came, deftly grabbing your phone and Face ID verifying

Yes, you really want to do this

before the

TMFWCAT just posted a photo

banner disappears into whatever ether said banners disappear to.

Todd looks confused—or would if you cared enough to look—but Todd can pretty much fuck right off because you're back on the emancipation-via-cyber-stalking case. You realize your heart rate is accelerated in anticipation, navigating to the social media platform he's posted to and wondering (accurately) if this is how a junkie feels seconds before the needle finds a vein and the Smack hits. One of those so-bad-it's-good-for-you sensations, washing over you with a sense of euphoria until

there's a new girl in his post

and the caption underneath says

My New Bitch

or something just like it.

The revelation comes faster than the banner that heralded the post that you looked at; the post that has now ruined your date/night/week/month/year/life the way it really, really shouldn't.

Your heart sinks; you realize—caption underneath unnecessary—from the way he's looking at her in the picture he's posted that she's different than all the other girls he's posted with.

You realize she's his new girlfriend.

You realize you're not okay with it.

...poor Todd.

CHAPTER TWELVE

His new bitch is ugly.

*and other lies you tell yourself.

*and me.

*and anyone who will listen.

thoughts for Thots.

Ugh.

She's hideous.

What does he see in her?

That whore.

With her fake lips and fake eyelashes and fake hair and fake tits and for-sure-fake fat ass.

What does she have that you don't

you ask yourself from your command post/bed, the place you've been operating from since Todd paid for that dinner that sucked and drove your sorry ass home.

And it might have been last night or three nights ago, and who the fuck cares anyways, your priorities and sense of self galvanized into a singular purpose:

Who does this bitch think she is?

Now, there is a part of you, deep deep down somewhere, that knows you should probably feel for this poor woman, caught as she is in his surely self-serving web. It's a primal, likely hormonal condition, this empathy for fellow vagina-havers—one that momentarily focuses your quiet rage back on him and his cocksure-smile-in-the-pic smiling smug-ass face. It is enough for you to consider reaching out to her in warning of the heartbreaks sure to befall her...and then you creep her open-to-the-public (slut) profile, and you find your ex-man all over it.

And you're back to wanting to drown a bitch.

...

Her name is unmentionable because you fucking hate her and because it's an admittedly trendier name than yours, her name so hot right now and likely, you tell yourself, because she's a goddamned post-millennial and so much younger than you.

You add

trendiness

to the hopefully-only-in-your-mind list of her flaws and faults, deflecting your hatred from where it most likely should be and decoding every subliminal message her social is trying to tell you.

She's got black hair, which you fucking hate, and only partly because your hair is decidedly *not* and only partly because he always swore he hated any hair color but yours.

And now you hate that you only worried about the blonde hoes at the bars he went out to, the realization that a bevy of brunette and raven-haired women had opportunities where you thought there were none.

Which has you replaying every night he came home late, filtering through all the boys who have let you down since, going back in your mind to some Tuesday or some

Saturday you're probably remembering all wrong and replaying the events of that evening through a new and impossibly distorted lens. Which now has you irrationally convinced that he was seeing this bitch the whole time—back when he was with you and after when he was posting pictures with women/dates that were oh-so-obviously fakes, a ruse to distract you from what was really going on all along.

Yeah, it makes total sense—the only logical reason he would ever rationally-or-ill break it off with a goddess like you is that this post-millennial whore clearly seduced him with her fake hair/lashes/lips/tits/ass. The more you explore/investigate her various social profiles, the more it makes sense; sure, the timelines don't reveal anything incriminating date-wise, but you're well aware of how deceptive/clever/tricky sidepieces can be—after all, wrecking homes/relationships is literally pre-requisite.

So you're diving deep on Becky (and no, that's unfortunately not her real name, but fuck her), and you're determining just how superior you are with every finger scroll but maybe believing it a little less with every pic you zoom in on.

She's impossibly pretty, there in the picture on the boat—but the armor your subconscious is erecting is lying to you and telling you that her big, beautiful green eyes are too far apart; that her freckles are tattooed on (and they very may well be, but they look amazing regardless) and that her perfectly perky breasts are anything other-than. The pic in the wheat field at sunset is laughably staged, sure—but you're fooling yourself into believing the thousands of others who double-tapped *like* are out of their collective minds; that the hundreds of comments are plants from what are so obviously burner accounts.

The fact that she has more followers than you is something to subvert also; your mind is already attributing *that* fact to *the* fact Becky must have been a prostitute. Must have been, or still is—you tell yourself that level of following doesn't come without spending a week or two as a Saudi-Arabian sex slave. You follow that thought down the line, picturing her hidden OnlyFans account and how photos of her doing horribly unspeakable acts likely contributed to this otherwise-inflated-by-bots number of devoted engagers.

You imagine hundreds of Fuckbois lusting after every scandalous addition to a smut-filled profile and how it had to have been platforms like this that stole your man away. You figure it is only logical that the next step was a profile on some Sugar Baby website, where she seduced men just like yours into paying her rent and buying her those trashy boots she's wearing in the latest picture you're staring at.

Yeah, she's a total skank, utilizing her beauty to get legions of followers and tons of money…you throw your phone onto the couch, disgusted at the thought of TMFWCAT falling for someone like that.

And then you pick your phone up two seconds later, realizing you could so *be* that skank.

CHAPTER THIRTEEN

OnlyFans.

thoughts for Thots.

Your username is ThotFineAss420, because why not.

It's your ass that first gave you the idea, posting that pic all those months ago, landing you the followers and the clout and the Fuckbois that inevitably led you *here*, OnlyFans and their latest-soon-to-be-greatest Influencer.

You have no idea what to charge for your monthly subscription/access to your body, so you start small, pictures and videos only $5.99 per month, a deal, and a good one given the content you plan on sharing.

You spend the rest of the afternoon creating content for that all-important first post. This requires a significant amount of work—there's laundry to be done, oil to be applied, lighting conditions to be made optimal. You're somewhat satisfied with your work some two-hundred-fifty-four photos later, creating the thirstiest content you possibly can, thumb shaking somewhat as you hit the upload button.

It goes live, your maiden post…and nothing happens.

Admittedly, you're used to the Instagram model, posting to your already somewhat established page and hashtagging appropriately, sitting back, and watching your thirst trap work its semi-erotic magic.

Realizing you're in uncharted territory, you decide that the anonymity of a fresh username isn't worth the apparent lack of attention your first post is getting/deserves; you decide to sacrifice the notion of hiding your inner hoe, and you post a link to your

OnlyFans account in your Instagram bio. (You realize Becky must have kept her account hidden, deviously engaging your ex-man first before referring him to her surely present page...but you're in a hurry, and fuck Becky.)

The attention comes somewhat slowly, too slowly to capitalize on what will undoubtedly be your ticket to the forefront of social media superstardom. Undeterred, you share your post from your newly-minted OnlyFans account to your Instagram, censoring this version by placing two (size-reduced) heart emojis over your nipples.

You transcribe something sassy,

Want more? Check out my OnlyFans

or

I've joined OnlyFans! Come play

or

You get to see my tits

or

something equally profound/deep. This post is submitted without the thumb shaking nervousness of the previous, and maybe you wonder why. Perhaps it's the familiarity with the platform; perhaps it's that you can tell yourself this isn't an upload to a site dedicated almost exclusively to pornography; hell, maybe it's the hearts-over-nipples. Regardless, you're remarkably more self-assured this go-round, pressing post and watching the overwhelmingly aggressive onslaught of likes/comments come in.

Your smartphone's poor little notification center is overworked almost immediately; satisfied in your success, you decide to retreat to the comforts of your bathtub, some seconds before the entrepreneur in you decides that you might as well record it.

. . .

The first week is productive, to say the least. You post two additional photos and a video—much to the delight of your steadily increasing subscriber base.

Sharing previews on your Instagram has exponentially accelerated your traffic to OnlyFans; updating the site's settings to include things like your Amazon Wishlist ensures that, while you wait for that first week's earnings to be accumulated/processed, you'll be benefitting from the perverts, acquaintances and casual-interest-with-disposable-income visitors via the gifts you've asked for. You've figured out the link to add streaming content; you decide only your top 5% of subscribers/gift-givers/tippers will earn that surely-forthcoming privilege.

The delight of the business opportunity is outweighing any hesitancy you've had regarding your naked body forever digestible online. Subsequently, each post has revealed a little more and reserved a little less. The trendline (one of the many business terms you've learned via Google) indicates the release of modesty has a direct correlation to an increase in earnings; as such, you're finding your Amazon Wishlist suddenly occupied with toys you'd otherwise have to enter a storefront with a frosted glass door pane to obtain.

You've stumbled onto a lucrative revenue stream; by the time you engage in your necessary next steps, you've forgotten to remember that the you of a week ago—the one convinced that Becky had stolen your ex-man—wouldn't recognize the you of right now, embracing your inner Thot, and about to celebrate others for the same behavior.

CHAPTER FOURTEEN

Their OnlyFans.

thoughts for Thots.

Your new day job—aside from taking naked pictures of yourself—is liking pictures of other Instagram Thots who have taken naked pictures of themselves.

Commenting on them too,

drool emoji

and

love! (heart emoji)

and

this set is so cute where is it from

even though you know goddamned well it's from FashionNova. Because every hoe bent over every couch is wearing FashionNova.

It's Instagram, and it's work, but you know that by networking with the community of like-minded Influencers, you'll receive new followers (from the mouth-breathers who read the comments) and, eventually, you'll receive similar shout-outs and comments from the established Thots you're now somewhat desperate to emulate.

It's good for you, in that you're spending less time obsessing over what went wrong with *this man* or *that man,* and you're spending less time scrutinizing women like Becky, and you're spending more time celebrating women like Becky.

You're subscribing—avidly—to other OnlyFans accounts, developing a taste for photography elements you'd never previously noticed and developing a taste for the beauty of the female body, and developing a taste for the power it holds over the vast majority of the male species.

You're filling a medium-sized notebook with concepts for photographs and names of relatively local photographers, and you're incredibly empowered by the creativity the endeavor is bringing out of you. You're appreciating the time black-haired Becky's and blonde-haired Ashley's have spent cultivating their respective brands; you're messaging both local and international Influencers, and you're absorbing every tip the ones who respond respond with.

One Ashley even suggests a collaborative coffee meeting; you're relatively sure that collaborative coffee meeting will turn into a collaborative filmed sexual act video, and you're relatively sure you're okay with that. You're on the cusp of some low-level tier of online superstardom. You figure a possible hookup with a similarly 'famous' online personality is safer than a possible hookup with a similarly 'famous' online person with a penis, so you agree to meet this Ashley (named Jessica) at a café across town.

collabs.

thoughts for Thots.

Jessica is mid-tier Instagram famous, and Jessica has an OnlyFans with hundreds of subscribers, and, in person, Jessica is stunningly beautiful.

Which is cool with you, saddling up to the chair opposite Jessica here at the trendy café you're meeting at because—according to Instagram and OnlyFans—you're stunningly beautiful also.

This meeting is non-threatening in a way online-derived in-person meetings with the Fuckbois you used to meet with were not. Regardless of whatever agenda Jessica may be looking to push, it's a mystery in the way every single Fuckbois' agenda was not. So while you introduce yourself the exact same way—a warm smile and an exaggerated bend at the waist to showcase your equally-impressive rack—you're sitting in the chair opposite Jessica, decidedly less afraid of what she may be about to propose.

It's sex.

Jessica's proposal for collaboration is sex, the way you kinda figured/hoped it would be. You're admittedly flattered and maybe even a little surprised with the ease in which she proposes it, proposing it as she does from across the café table in between sips of something you can't help but notice she looks good sipping.

She's attractive in the way Influencers of her ilk

sometimes-always are; you can't tell if you're attracted to her because she's attractive or if you're attracted to her because of the business associating her established brand with your burgeoning brand will generate. Either way, you're interested; it might be in the sex with someone of distinctly different gender, and it might be in the possibility women in relationships might bring. You tell Jessica

why not

and after six drinks and four hours, you agree to meet her at her studio/studio apartment across town next Friday night.

...

You're nervous, and you're excited, and you're shaking a little, emerging from the Uber you would have found expensive were you not here and about to make a great deal of money.

The elevator ride to Jessica's studio/studio apartment is longer than the thirteen-floor ride you're used to; you spend the entirety of the ride analyzing yourself in the mirror. You're dressed at least as well as you would have for a first date. The acknowledgment of the butterflies and the recognition of their presence on dates, too, have you smiling as you exit the elevator on the top floor.

Jessica's *penthouse* apartment is ostentatious and gaudy and wonderful. She welcomes you with a warm hug and a glass of champagne; you're suddenly so enamored with her beauty that you fail to notice the Louis Vuitton rug she nearly trips over on her way to embrace you. You're well into your second champagne flute by the time the tour has ended; you're marveling at the opulence OnlyFans can provide, and you're amazed that studio/studio apartments on penthouse floors can be *this* big.

She ends the tour in her celebrated/aforementioned studio—a converted bedroom bigger than your cozy little one-bedroom apartment bathed in brilliant halo lighting and appointed with enough camera technology to rival a small city's newsroom. You settle into a sofa she tells you is from some store you've never heard of, and it's made of some leather you can't pronounce; it's comfortable and maybe a little *too,* and Jessica is cuddled up next to you, and your champagne glass is filled for the third time in an hour, and your thoughts are racing faster than this sentence and before you know it...

CHAPTER SIXTEEN

In over your head.

thoughts for Thots.

...there is a ball gag in your mouth.

It's okay because it's consensual, it's okay because it was all part of Jessica's plan, and it's okay because this whole light-BDSM thing is kind of fun.

Painful, with the whole wooden paddle intermittently exploding across the skin of your tender little ass cheeks thing...but fun. You cry out, kinda, elaborating for the cameras but stifled somewhat by the annoying ball gag in your mouth. The drool is the worst part, falling overly consistently and temporarily staining the designer rug you're on all-fours atop. Jessica seems to mind, but she's sworn it's just for the filming you're in the middle of filming, and she promises the video you'll subsequently share across your socials will make you the kind of famous a little pain is worth.

So the mock humiliation she suggested after her fourth champagne glass is humiliating. Still, you've seen enough pornography and known enough perverts to understand the market for this kind of thing. Still, there are surprises in your asshole (all of a sudden) that make you remind yourself of the money you're sure to make—you squeal in surprise and pain, and you reassure yourself it is all part of the process. You go to some safe place in your head, submitting to the rhythm of the paddling and thinking back two champagne glasses ago when Jessica promised you'd have full control of how much of this virtual submission goes out to the fans. One champagne glass ago, she extolled the virtues of live streaming—despite the glow the bubbles had given you, you'd decided you're still far from comfortable with footage like this going out with no opportunity to edit heavily. She had laughed, Jessica, telling you something about eventualities—in the moment, now, you're forgiven for not remembering details given what's going on.

Somewhere behind you, Jessica is doing horribly experimental things to you; she's calling you the kinds of names you suppose a master calls a slave and—despite her prior assurances it's all a well-intentioned act—you can't help but feel she's getting a kick out of hiding the heel of her ridiculously-priced pump in your softest of parts.

. . .

After the filming is over, you shower at Jessica's apartment, and at her behest, she films the showering. She's assured you that capturing content for future releases is of the most importance; you're too drunk and maybe too submissive from the 'mock' beating she's just given you, and so you step into the shower at her request/command.   You're lathering and reflecting, trying to scan your memories of the very recent past as to whether or not you enjoyed this collaboration the way you'd wanted to.

You're sure you're sore, and you're sure your heart is still racing—just as you're feeling the first unmistakable pang of loneliness, not alone in Jessica's master bathroom, Jessica is in the shower and behind you and holding you the way you've only just realized you really need her to.

The water is warm, and so is her embrace and, long before you climb into her unnecessarily large California King bed, you're grateful for the girl, if not the voyeuristic sex.

...

She makes you breakfast, only after wrapping you in what she calls her favorite Versace robe, holding your hand, and escorting you to the patio of the penthouse studio/studio apartment you're already feeling comfortable in.

The eggs are running the way your mascara did last night; you're picking at the toast and fighting both the hangover and the wealth of emotion swirling around in your head. Had you the time, you might recognize the unease you feel when she's away from you—you're about to, and then Jessica is beside you again, humming softly to the Top 40 hit suddenly playing from her phone after kissing you softly on her way to the seat next to you.

It gives you pause, her kiss, the first of its kind not disguised as theatre for fans and subscribers who've yet to discover it. The warmth on her lips is a sharp contrast to the hate in her voice during last night's performance; after enjoying her kiss and the kisses that follow, you return to your eggs and the suspicion that—when it comes to all things Jessica—you might be in over your head.

CHAPTER SEVENTEEN

Angels with dirty faces.

thoughts for Thots.

The video—edited to your somewhat reserved approval—goes out to your OnlyFans sometime the next afternoon. Jessica shares it over her socials also—to say it does well is an understatement. Having just received your very first payout from the site—minus the twenty percent hosting fee—you're well aware of what you can expect come the next seven to ten days and paycheque number two.

Jessica suggests you celebrate, her heavily-eyeshadowed fucking seafoam green eyes radiating at the proposal. You're lost in them, her eyes, and the intoxication that comes from earning the type of money your OnlyFans activity swears you're about to.

So it's shopping and drinks, but only after holding Jessica at least as tight as you can and only after kissing her until the breath absent your body demands you take one.

She dresses you in a dress that really just pretends; it's tight and too, and it accentuates the uncomfortable your traffic suggests shouldn't be uncomfortable anymore. Jessica warns you against raising your arms above shoulder level—unless, she confirms, you want your nipples out—and she scoffs at your attempt to hide panties underneath what must be Lycra material. You take them off at her behest, and you let her play with where they just came from at her behest, and you don't even question the pill she places on your tongue after her tongue leaves it, and you don't even question the fact that this could be the start of your latest, significant problem.

The Uber takes you somewhere, and it might as well be at lightspeed because whatever pill you've taken has got you tripping balls. She's singing to the radio or the driver is singing to the radio, or the singer from the radio is singing to the song on the radio from the passenger seat. You can't tell because you're high, and you don't care because Jessica is holding you in the backseat of the Uber, and you can feel the warmth of her skin.

Because just about all of it is out, her mini-dress somehow more mini than yours, it looking better on her, pretty much the last coherent thought you thought before thoughts became anything but.

The Uber drives/flies your spaceship to some pre-arranged destination. You climb out to the best of your admittedly limited ability, laughing with Jessica at the sudden revelation that you've revealed your vagina and your anus to the driver and anyone on the bustling boulevard you've arrived at. She says something about it kinda being your thing now, Jessica does, emerging onto the street behind you and accidentally/not revealing even more.

She's a vision, all tasteful piercings, and tasteful tattoos, and, staring at her under the streetlight you stumble to, you're realizing that you're falling very quickly under the same spell you assume most of her nine-hundred-twenty-nine-thousand Instagram followers have. She looks at you with those fucking seafoam green eyes, and you feel your heart skip the way it hasn't since TMFWCAT was just TMFYRWILW. (The Mother Fucker You

Really Were In Love With.) The drugs tell you she can read your mind, and maybe that is true because just before you came to the realization you love her after less than two weeks of knowing her, Jessica is grabbing you by the hand and leading you to the first pre-shopping bar she swears is mandatory.

Those thoughts are better reserved for times when thoughts aren't heavily influenced by heavy narcotics; she leads you to some reserved booth, and you slide in, safe like some ballplayer sliding into second base. You go to second base right there in the booth, waiting for cocktails and suddenly appreciating Jessica's insistence that panties were a distinct no.

Your head is swirling, and the first of several drinks to arrive goes down smooth; before you know it, you're shopping with newly earned money, and for the first time in your life, you're buying clothes specifically because the price tag is ridiculous. Jessica is both the proverbial angel on your shoulder (reassuring you that you can afford it) and the proverbial devil on your shoulder (reminding you there'll be things going in your ass to ensure you can continue to afford it); you're still buzzing by the time you exit your eighth store with at least that many thousand spent.

Your high is fading just enough to tell you the bags you're burdened with are becoming overwhelmingly heavy. Jessica puts your awakening, troubled mind at ease, reassuring you that her bags are heavy, too, and that it's time for your dinner reservation. By the time you walk to the restaurant she maybe lied when she told you was close, you're exhausted, and there is a headache settling in where your high used to be. You're analyzing the gluttony of purchases you've made and beginning to regret at least all of them as the well-dressed hostess ushers you to your table. You're coming up with a plan to return two pairs of the Louboutin pumps, barely surveying the landscape of the seemingly packed, over-dark dining room when you're snapped to reality with the proverbial force of one of Jessica's paddles across your ass.

The hostess signals you've arrived at your table, which wouldn't be out of the ordinary, save the fact there are two men seated at it. You expect Jessica to remind the hostess that the reservation was for two, and you expect the hostess to blush and utter

my mistake

and you expect her to escort you to your waiting, suitably-vacant table hurriedly. What you don't expect is the squeal of excited glee to escape Jessica's perfectly enhanced/suddenly parted lips. You don't expect her breasts to come spilling from the top of her too-mini mini dress as she commits the cardinal sin of raising her perfectly tattooed arms above her shoulders, reaching as she reaches to embrace the clearly-not-a-stranger seated at (what you realize to your dismay is) your table.

The hostess leaves, clearly satisfied in helping you reach what is unfortunately/clearly your table; you're left awkwardly standing as both of the mysterious/heavily-scented men rise to hug Jessica and Jessica's exposed nipples and rise, you suppose, to hug you too.

They do, hug you, and their overpowering colognes are matched only by their overpowering, overly friendly greetings. You're relatively sure the larger of them grabs your ass sometime mid-hug; the headache and the overhearing that they're

your biggest fans

has you reeling for the first time since the drugs had you reeling some four hours ago. You forgive yourself for not really catching their names during the following seating/introduction; you're trying to focus on Jessica's explanation that the smaller man owns a textile factory and that the larger one has been her most avid/loyal supporter.

You weigh this and the small talk that follows against your admittedly distorted recollection of the events of the past few hours, scanning your brain against electrical impulses to smile where appropriate and act as though you're not totally caught off guard. You finish your memory scan and realize

no

Jessica had not mentioned anything about two hairy, seemingly pervy men joining you at dinner and

no

you think you'd remember flagging such a proposition as a pretty decisive fuck-no.

So you're sitting at a table for four instead of sitting at the table for two you'd agreed to, headache pounding and buzz wearing off beside/across two wealthy/powerful men you're quickly realizing have some very real expectations for what is to go down post-dinner.

...

You escape to the ladies' room the first chance you can, wresting your hand from the smaller man's invasive grasp and declarations that he's never seen a woman as beautiful as you. You're trying to focus, staring at yourself in the bathroom mirror and you're debating leaving your ridiculously-priced purchases at the table and behind, should you dart out the back door when Jessica walks into the bathroom behind you.

You give her your best

what the fuck are you doing

are you fucking crazy

but her fucking seafoam green eyes are disarming you, and her perfectly-enhanced lips are parting to explain some sweet-sounding nonsense about how

they just really wanted to meet you

and

this is a great opportunity for you

and

this is part of the deal.

You're having flashbacks to the part of the deal that had you on all fours over Jessica's ridiculously priced rug, and you're reminded that the limits of your comfort with 'the deal' were reached right around the time that first vibrator went inside of your anus. You temper your reaction as best you can (which, given the state you're in, your reaction probably isn't very tempered), and Jessica is listening/scanning your eyes with her fucking seafoam green eyes, and just before you get to the part where you're angry at her for deceiving/luring you into some weird sex proposition, she's kissing you with those perfectly enhanced lips.

You're confused and reeling, and you push her away— but only just far enough to make your point, all

how could you

and

what kind of weird orgy are these assholes expecting

before

did they pay you for this?

She pauses, held there at the end of your still-embrace, and she takes in the last of your admittedly frantic line of questions/accusations, and you're expecting her to react poorly/the way the asshole men in your past surely would have reacted to an outburst like this.

Instead, she just smiles that disarming smile, and she assures you that she'll call you an Uber and that she'll tell the men you're not feeling well and that she'll help you load your litany of purchases and that you should sleep it off at her penthouse studio/studio apartment.

You hold her tightly again, kissing her lips earnestly between the bevy of

thank you

thank you

-s (plural) you throw her way.

Minutes later, you're stepping awkwardly into the Uber and, between attempts at adjusting your revealed bits and settling amongst a backseat full of ridiculously priced items, you stop to wonder why Jessica's last words were

I'll see you tomorrow

and

just where the hell she plans on spending her night tonight.

CHAPTER EIGHTEEN

Upgrades.

thoughts for Thots.

Jessica has fake hair. (Glue-ins.)

Jessica has fake eyelashes. (Mink.)

Jessica has fake cheekbones. (Collagen injections.)

Jessica has a new nose. (Plastic surgery #1.)

Jessica has fake tits. (Plastic surgeries #2 and #3.)

Jessica has had her floating ribs removed. (!)

Jessica has a fake fat ass. (Fat injections, which she tells you is the best/safest way.)

Listening to Jessica detail the various procedures she's undergone to become the desirable Influencer/mogul she has become, you're looking in the mirror, and you're thinking you could use an upgrade also.

In the week since your first submission video went live on OnlyFans (both yours and hers), the traffic to your subscription-based site has skyrocketed. You're seven days into a seven-to-ten day request for your earnings, after which—thanks to Jessica promoting your brand— you're going to receive the biggest paycheque of your young life. Enough to pay for the litany of upgrades you—until very recently—weren't aware you so desperately needed.

In the days that followed her probable attempt to force you into an orgy with two highly-engaged fans, Jessica— since returning the following morning looking rougher than you could have possibly imagined—has rarely left your side. You've spent the bulk of your time in her penthouse studio/studio apartment, steadily-strategically planning content creation and, now, steadily-strategically planning plastic surgery. She assures you that her surgeon is the best surgeon and books you a consultation; analyzing your naked body in the mirror, she assures you that her tattoo artist is the best tattoo artist, and she books you a consultation.

Girls with plentiful ink earn more, she says, something about appealing to multiple demographics before muttering something about engaging in multiple kinks. You're so busy picturing your curves covered in colors that you only half-hear; as with the majority of Jessica's darker-intentioned comments/acts, you opt to pretend they don't penetrate your ears/anus.

...

You're seated in the surgeon's office less than a week later, freshly-paid, and having spent the better part of the week that was living with Jessica and sleeping with Jessica and creating content with Jessica. This, Jessica assures you, will be enough to keep your OnlyFans page updated while you recover from what the surgeon tells you will be (conservatively) months of recovery time. He also tells you he's booked solid for the next foreseeable future (the way the receptionist icily told you he's booked for the next foreseeable future), but Jessica and her fucking seafoam green eyes are batting away beside you and hypnotizing/convincing him that the window from this consultation to the day you wake up with titties and ass decidedly bigger than when you went to sleep should be shorter than what she admits is her really short level of patience. Her short dress helps encourage him to make haste, so the appointment, he assures, won't be long in the waiting.

You're happy she tagged along, vouching for you from her chair beside the doctor's bed you awkwardly sit on, topless and allowing the surgeon to examine your breasts for what must be the best point of entry. Which turns out to be your armpits, but that's not the point—the point is that the surgeon is continually/affectionately referring to Jessica as his favorite client, and he's matter-of-factly stating that her breasts turned out perfectly. You take note that—unlike so many of the men you've met via Jessica—the surgeon is in no way creepy or pervy or aggressive. The picture of his loving family visible from over his left shoulder suggests this is an appointment lacking any agenda other than blowing up what you're now lovingly referring to as your money-makers.

Jessica and the surgeon go back and forth about their personal preferences for the appropriate size of your future-tits; you're with him, and his suggestion that you remain somewhat conservative and a mere three cup sizes greater. You realize Jessica is now batting her fucking seafoam green eyes at you and bartering for something a little more ridiculous. You're increasingly worried this attempt at the final say will go the way of a larger injection of fat into your ass (her idea) and the combination of surgeries on the same day (health screen passed, of course—why have two separate recovery times—her idea) and what looks to be a decidedly shorter wait time than that bitch at the front desk had warned you about.

You're sensing a pattern; the same pattern you'd had at the *other* plastic surgeon's office you'd visited this week—the one when you went in for a slight increase in lip size and left with collagen in your lips and cheekbones and jawline and Botox in your forehead and under your eyes.

She'd calmed you down, post-injections, with ice cream and Netflix and chill—watching her work her manipulative little magic, you're wondering what treats await you after this conversation.

…

You leave the surgeon's office with a date, and it is soon; soon, like your first appointment with the tattoo artist, his waitlist impacted directly and as well by Jessica's subtle persuasions. It turns out that the next few months promise a significant amount of both alterations and pain—as you nervously rub the naked-but-not-for-long skin of your arm, you're wondering where the combination of this wild mentor/lover and your emergence as a kind of social media sex star will take you next.

CHAPTER NINETEEN

New You.

thoughts for Thots.

Your tits hurt, and your ass hurts, and your arm hurts, and the freshly-tattooed area just beneath/between your newly augmented breasts hurts too. You'd put your foot down at Jessica's suggestion for floating rib removal—lying in her ridiculous California King bed and hurting from head to toe, you're glad you did.

The drugs the surgeon provided are helping; they're also working hard to obscure your recollection of the conversation pre-op. The one where the surgeon exchanged heated words with Jessica regarding what you insisted was your decision to tattoo an area so close to an area about to be affected by elective surgery. He was defeated on his suggestion to postpone the top half of the top/bottom enhancement by Jessica's fucking persuasive fucking seafoam green eyes and by your less persuasive eyes and more persuasive waiver signings.

So you're twice as sore, major surgeries completed and, lying in Jessica's ridiculous California King bed, the only thing easing your pain (aside from Jessica and her admittedly awesome bedside manner) is counting the subscribers, followers, and fans to your monetized and non-monetized socials.

You've requested the coveted Instagram 'blue check,' a symbol of authentic celebrity-esque status, at Jessica's behest and after seeing a half-dozen (and counting) fake accounts pretending to be you and showcasing what is—unbeknownst to all of them—your now *old* ass. You're flattered, to a point, by the more ridiculous of them, bios suggesting 'you' would message every new follower and links to paid accounts that aren't paying you, and so they're reported by you as fake, flattery be damned.

You're ruling an empire while you convalesce, absorbing every insight shared by your ahead-by-less-than-a-dozen followers (now) mentor, her companionship/online dominance paving the way for you never to need a real/shitty job ever again. So you're eternally grateful, and you're eternally indebted (because you'll never be in debt again) and, although you feel you'll be eternally sore, Jessica and the prescription pain pills suggest otherwise.

Until then, it's Netflix and champagne but only after pills and hours of strategically planning the previously filmed uploads that will guarantee to grow your net worth while you get used to your newly grown ass and titties.

…

It might be the pain, and it might be the pills, and it might be the distinct lack of sleep followed by the bouts of delirium, but you swear Jessica comes and goes often during your recuperation. The absent days began innocently enough (to the best of your admittedly limited recollection). Her comings and goings more attributed to drug store runs and other excursions that benefitted you directly. As your healing progressed, her durations of time away seemed to progress accordingly—sometime around recovery week three, she spent the first of what would turn out to be *many* nights away. These, of course, were more concretely memorable due to the lack of a warm body curled tightly beside/around you—a missing element you could argue as key to your pain management.

When Jessica returns, she returns with gifts; gifts maybe equally key to your pain management, and so Jessica's absences—while noted—are forgiven and not questioned, her presence in bed beside you proving enough to ease your troubled mind. She curls in bed beside you tonight, and for the first time in two nights or three nights—the pills tell you that you can't tell for sure—and you fall asleep worrying less about where she's been and thinking more about where your social media traffic is going, once you make your new-you debut.

...

You do—debut—some weeks later and with a welcome-back Instagram post appropriately titled 'welcome back.' The post contains multiple photos, and in the multiple photos, you're displaying your newly-augmented physique in a variety of increasingly-thirsty-with-every-right-swipe examples of just how much you appreciate your loyal followers and just where their OnlyFans donations went. You're sufficiently healed and hell-bent on making up for lost time, linking your paywall-restricted profile in the accompanying caption and promising you'll be uploading uncensored versions of the barely-censored content there and almost immediately.

Judging by the likes and accompanying comments, your audience is in favor of your new frame; for every comment on your freshly-healed tattoos there are two appreciating your newly-juicy lips and five appreciating your newly-juicy titties, and ten appreciating your newly-juicy ass.

You're addicted to the pills, the way they numb the pain that isn't really there anymore, and you're addicted to the validation—every comment coming through reminding you that, by embracing your inner Thot and by investing the proceeds of the initial 'I'm a Thot' campaign into what you now understand were necessary augmentations, your new life is tens of thousands of followers better than your old life.

CHAPTER TWENTY

Cam girl.

thoughts for Thots.

It's the logical progression for you, Jessica says.

It's a different level of connectivity, Jessica says, and Jessica says connectivity is the key to maximizing revenue generation with your (now) legions of adoring fans.

Jessica says something about brand diversification, and it sounds good, and it makes sense, so you listen to Jessica the way you're only just beginning to realize you always do. She ties the launch of your streaming/cam girl channel to your debut as an over-sexed, over-sculpted, over-enhanced online deity; playing to your vanity the way you both realize is the key to coercion---after all, vanity is the key to your money, also.

You tour all of the requisite major players— Chaturbate.com, Pornhub's PornLive.com—before settling on myfreecams.com, and not only because it is 'The Number One Adult Webcam Community.' Jessica's channel is hosted there, and—after some shady dealings with other hosting sites—she's beyond impressed with the tokens to cash conversion/payout system. The top models, she tells you, earn over forty-thousand per month; judging by the state of the penthouse studio/studio apartment you're laid up researching in, she's among them.

She facilitates the conversation with the appropriate administrators the way she facilitates most of the important-figure-for-your-future conversations, and— within a week—you're set up in her incredibly equipped penthouse studio/studio apartment about to broadcast for the very first time. You're nervous—the better part of the past week spent direct messaging your most loyal followers and offering them access to this 'soft launch.' You know this doesn't necessarily guarantee they'll pay to support you on this new platform, many of them paying a premium on another. You promise this will be even more revealing (wondering if such a thing is remotely possible) and leaning heavily on Jessica's promise for unparalleled activity.

Thoughts of putting yourself out there, literally and live, and not having tokens virtually thrown your way are weighing uncomfortably on your mind, the remote-controlled vibrator weighing equally uncomfortably from its new home in your vagina. This whole undertaking is starting to feel sleazier, somehow, than the pre-recorded beatings/sex you've begrudgingly become accustomed to. You shift your weight to avoid the emerging physical discomfort, and the plastic living inside of you reminds you why your feelings aren't solely metaphorical.

Distracting you with her beauty and her nudity from behind the elaborate camera/laptop setup, Jessica begins the pre-established ten-second countdown. Having recently been standing—literally—in her place, you'd hoped the afternoon you'd just spent watching her interact with her fans would have prepared you for this somewhat pivotal moment.

As the countdown finishes and the recording light explodes red from across the room, you realize it did not.

. . .

You start slow.

You watch the laptop screen count your audience members, and you do your best to introduce yourself to the

67 people

instantly tuned into this, your first live performance.

Jessica had told you that many would be fans from your Instagram and OnlyFans platforms—that visitors happening by the host site would be given a menu of performing-live 'rooms,' but that established performers would be given priority designation at the top of the screen. The key, she said, to attract new fans with no prior knowledge is the screenshot your room profile allowed—and that the more scandalous the pic, the more attractive the profile. Given the

73 people

now watching you stumble through your introduction, you chose well. Like a strip-show, the key to a successful cam show is starting slow—often clothed, albeit in something provocative—and offering a menu of interactive performance 'milestones' for your viewers to reach given their cumulative tokens.

You wouldn't call the pink tape over your nipples, criss-crossed into a letter 'x' particularly tantalizing, but then again, you're not a pink nipple tape kind of girl. Jessica, apparently, is, and so the first of your many planned reveals will be doing your very best to remove it without causing the kind of pain you're worried you're spending way too much of this important moment focusing on.

New visitor Biggstuddd43 asks

how many tokens to see your nipples

succeeding in both keeping your mind on how much peeling off the fucking tape is going to hurt and validating Jessica's statement that despite the clearly labeled

125 tokens flash

menu item just underneath the live image of you and your pink titties, many of your fans will be too mesmerized to read.

Unless, it seems, it involves reading other fan's comments. User Kush2342 reminds Biggstuddd43 exactly where he can go to be encouraged in token-parting.

User SkeletonKey chimes in also, calling Biggstuddd43 a fucking moron and validating another of Jessica's educational statements; that you should take your time and read comments, often aloud, to encourage participation and, more importantly, because reading comments is over half the fun.

The other half of the fun—the fun Jessica was adamant

about you having to get used to—kicks in violently as Biggstuddd43 (clearly having read the menu) pays the 100 tokens to activate your vibrator.

It stops you mid-sentence; all of a sudden, your verbal

thank you

to SkeletonKey's claim that you have the best titties on the internet turns into

thank yofffuuuuccckk

because the only part of you not yet revealed to the

92 people

watching your broadcast just experienced the Level Two setting of your Lovense brand vibrator.   Jessica mentioned   (in   her   usual,   nonchalant-borderline-dismissive-focus-on-my-fucking-seafoam-green-eyes kind of way) that you had nothing to worry about until Level Five; having skipped Level One, you're instantly terrified of both pink nipple tape and the power of the pink toy nestled way too far up your pussy.

103 people

are appreciating your sex-faced uncomfortable reaction; you're fighting to find the

stop

or

wait

or

no more tokens

words that would probably-not-but-worth-a-shot stop SkeletonKey and Biggstuddd43 and LoverBoyXX2 and fucking Rad Chad the TikTok personality you went on that Fuckboi date with from tipping the way they are, essentially having sex with you from the comfort of their proverbial parent's basements.

…

An hour later, the ordeal—and really, that is the most appropriate term for what you have just subjected yourself to—is over. You did your very best to engage in conversation with the

203 people

who combined to view your stream at its peak, right before your (second) peak due to the contribution of their collective contributions. As Jessica signals that the Livestream is officially over, you shudder off the effects of your second orgasm, and you do your best to remember the events of the hour after your vagina began vibrating uncontrollably. You're sure that you must have looked ridiculous, unable to form a coherent thought, let alone sentences, when the Lovense hit Level 5; your ability to see the comments on the screen gone long before the collective realized your reactions to their tokens tipping ensured they should keep you buzzing.

Thoughts of debasing yourself for the gratification of the unwashed masses doesn't turn you on the way the thoughts of the unwashed masses tipping you handsomely does. Jessica tackles you with an overly enthusiastic bear hug, her unintelligible squeal translating approval for your first show's earnings. Your back lands on some ridiculously-expensive shag carpet, and it does little to stop the pain shooting up from between your legs, reminding you as the glow of satisfaction fades that the object between your legs is foreign and pressing against places comfort dictates it just shouldn't be.

You politely excuse yourself, surviving Jessica's barrage of kisses and writhing your way off of the carpet. You lock the bathroom door, wincing as your remove the source of your present pain and your past pleasure, and your future earnings. Sitting on the bathroom floor, it takes the attempted opening of your Instagram messages to note two very important details:

You haven't stopped shaking

and

the amount of new followers and new Direct Messages on your social feeds that are commenting on your performance tells you that you'll never be able to keep your platforms separate again.

CHAPTER TWENTY ONE

When 'next logical steps' aren't really logical at all.

thoughts for Thots.

More is more

is what Jessica is always saying

and

more

is what you spend the better part of the next few weeks doing. You're fully healed, if not fully confident, but the money you're making from OnlyFans is trumped only by the money you're making from myfreecams.com, and that, Jessica assures you, can be trumped also. On this, she's intentionally vague, and so you settle (as best you can) into a cadence of photoshoot afternoons and live cam show evenings, adjusting to the admittedly continual discomfort of having something foreign between your legs dictate when you get off.

And so getting off is both something you do uncomfortably often and getting off is something you rarely do, every day and every night seemingly spent naked or close to it and for—judging by the traffic—everybody's benefit.

Everybody but Jessica, it seems, her nightly absences increasing in regularity. You're confident that you can run the cam show, if not entirely sure you can survive it—missing her is becoming more about going to bed alone than wondering where she runs off to while you're filming.

The studio part of her penthouse studio/studio

apartment keeps you here in her absence; your cozy little one-bedroom apartment fast becoming a place you pay for monthly and barely remember.

You're earning enough for a small palace of your own—despite her semi-regular nocturnal activities, you remain resigned to the possibility she *could* spend the night holding you to the idea of sleeping in some bed attached to someplace she doesn't belong.

And so you stay, sleeping alone literally after sleeping with (virtually) the

347 people

stroking themselves to the idea of being able to reach through the computer screen and do more than tip you for the fantasy.

All

347 people

are treated to the sight of you on all fours tonight, your modesty gone and out the front door the way Jessica went some half-hour before the tiny red light on the camera pointed directly at your asshole blinked on.

You reckon it's amazing what you can get used to, Level 3 buzzing away, not deterring your thoughts from thoughts of Jessica and from thoughts of your current situation and not the current situation that has you twerking violently to the sounds of tokens cling-clinging on the laptop behind you. You're riding some existential wave, catching a glimpse of your newly-enhanced naked body writhing on the computer screen, and noting how quickly you've become comfortable with whoring your digital self for copious amounts of cash.

...

Whore your physical self for copious amounts of cash

Jessica says,

says without saying it while saying something that sounds just like it.

You're sitting across the table from her at some ridiculously priced restaurant, a ridiculously priced restaurant just like the one you ran away from the last time Jessica sort of proposed sex with fans.

Those fans were present, and the fans she's proposing sex with are present only by the examples she's laying out, but your initial reaction is pretty much the same. You recoil in your chair, physical reaction to her answer regarding just where in the hell she's been these increasingly frequent nights away.

You expected a boyfriend or a tryst with a married man who couldn't be a boyfriend based on marital status, or you expected (another) girlfriend when you casually asked her to dinner to not-so-casually investigate where she's been. You didn't expect her casual

I've been having sex for money

casual-ass answer.

The fact that she follows that shocker up with

You should be having sex with fans for money

has you wishing you had more chair to recoil into. There's no more chair, but there are pills; you reach into your ridiculously expensive purse, and you curse your nervously fumbling fingers, furiously sorting through ridiculously expensive makeups and hand lotions until you find what you're searching for—your mercifully re-filled prescription of plastic surgery numbing pain pills. You pop a handful, washing it down with a half-glass of wine and hoping the cumulative effects kick in fast—fast and enough to numb the influence of Jessica's fucking seafoam green eyes, burning their way into your soul and directly through whatever rational ability you possess to deny her.

You brush off her follow up statement,

You should be having sex for money

spoken exactly the same way and somehow hitting harder, offering her your best

with who

instead. You meant to ask

who have you been having sex with

and so her response is long and detailed and filled with

specifics; names of your biggest supporters and examples of how to solicit them, and suggestions as to how much to collect for incredibly specific services rendered.

She manages to say all of this in what feels like a minute, speaking in her hurriedly excited squeaky-voiced Jessica way, somehow sneaking in healthy hits of wine and still elaborating on concepts you did not know you needed to hear.

She's selling you, even though the wine warns you

she's selling you

and the pills chime in with

just wait, we haven't kicked in yet.

They're about to, and you sincerely hope your presence in the here and now is faded and fast, the slow burn realization that your girlfriend/mentor might very well be adding *slash* pimp onto that prestigious list.

Not that she's asking for a cut, wildly gesturing as the point to her beautifully-illustrated rant is reached; sitting in silent-somewhat-shock, you can't rationalize whether you're shocked or shocked you didn't see this coming.

If the wine and the pills allowed for perspective, you might realize it's the cash that has blinded you; the freedom of removal from financial burden and the beauty of the one who introduced you to it sheltering you from the fact that it took being bent over with something up your asshole to achieve it. (While she beat you with a paddle—but specific details are rapidly fading like details in general, your focus on the warmth emanating from the hole you shoved the stimulants and depressants and pain relaxers down.)

The shocking elements of what probably shouldn't be a shocking conversation are fading like your care for them, replaced by the warmth of the breeze from the open restaurant window and the warmth of the enthusiasm radiating from the goddess across the table steering the conversation the way she tends to.

You're along for the ride, waves of positivity slowly churning in the forefront of what was recently a troubled mind; you contribute to the conversation when decorum allows, genuinely interested in the stories of where she's been and who she's been fucking for money—the way, you're realizing—you're likely about to.

...

CHAPTER TWENTY TWO

GFE.

thoughts for Thots.

You're having sex for money.

Back up a bit—you didn't just blink your pretty-but-not-fucking-seafoam-green eyes and end up *here*, riding Biggstuddd43 (while focusing those eyes on anything but the bloated body gyrating furiously beneath you), in the admittedly-expensive hotel room you admittedly-instantly regretted showing up to.

That was before the first of two bottles he offered and opened, back when you found his nervous enthusiasm cute—or at least back when you told yourself you found it cute, anything to mix with the bubbles and the pills you knew it would take to fuck him.

And you are—fucking him—and it's the creepy/horrible you were worried it would be. Jessica talked you into it the way Jessica always seems to talk you into it, assurances of sexually transmitted disease screens and non-disclosure agreements and insisting that many of the token-contributing, OnlyFans tipping whales like Biggstuddd43 were aware of the standard operating procedure for proceedings like this.

It turns out BiggStuddd43—or Todd, as it happens, so he's Todd2--was aware of the necessary protocols; his STD tests came back negative, and he signed the NDA within 24 hours of Jessica emailing it off to him on your behalf. Attached to the email with the NDA was a signed copy of the bill of sale—you hated that term the first time you saw it and, riding Todd2's decidedly not Biggstuddd cock, you hate it now, too. The money agreed to upon it, however, was enough to get you into the limo Jessica rented/Todd2 paid for and enough to get you on the elevator up to this admittedly expensive hotel room and enough to get you to not run away when he opened the door to the room you find yourself fucking in.

Before—before the fucking unmercifully still occurring—you told yourself that his bashfulness was something close to cute and certainly more welcome than any modicum of aggression in light of money paid. You humored him, pretending to be interested when he toured the admittedly impressive hotel room and when he explained that—despite his relatively easy maneuvering of the negotiations associated with this sort of transaction—that this was his first time, too.

You remind yourself, mid-ride, to give Jessica hell for sharing with Todd2 that this was your maiden voyage, momentarily interrupting your mental recapping of the events that led you here with the grim realities associated with your unfortunately-still-occurring series of events somewhat still occurring beneath you.

Todd2 has stamina, somehow, making the most of his moment with what he kept describing as 'the love of his life.' You found that to be the kind of creepy it really is, and yet the money paid for services rendered required the 'services rendered' part, and so you let him fumble through undressing you. His kisses—when you finally permitted him to kiss you—tasted like the champagne you guzzled to make kissing Todd2 anything close to okay, trying now not to retch, thinking of what else you're likely about to guzzle. Because where Todd2 finishes was a big part of the aforementioned agreement, specific geography acquiesced to so long as said geography was nowhere remotely close to inside you.

Judging by the look on Todd2's face (red as the bottoms of the Louboutins you're envisioning buying exciting you in place of the excitement this exchange is supposed to), he's a moment or two from violating the terms of his agreement.

You're off him in a flash, the motion disagreeing with the bubbles in your system and leaving you dizzy and seeking refuge on the small bed space not occupied by a startled, convulsing Todd2. He erupts—as you'd so critically calculated—moments later, his excitement and elation physically manifested in the semen about to pour all over him.

Remembering the dollar signs attached to his (situation fitting) disappointing amount of excretion, you endeavor to maneuver your face and chest directly under the still-falling projectile. Your level of drunk makes it difficult, but you manage to catch the last of it on your chin, wincing as you feel the hot splash cascade across your skin.

You allow Todd2 to admire his handiwork for what feels like an eternity, finally excusing yourself to the well-appointed washroom and turning the shower on to the hottest possible temperature. You hear Todd2 call out from the bed, something about wanting to watch. It takes every fiber of your being not to tell him to fuck off, relenting reluctantly and disappearing into the quickly rising steam before he can plod his way into your view.

You close your eyes as tightly as you can, scrubbing yourself furiously and doing your best to ignore the *fap fapping* of Todd2 pleasuring himself to your much-needed cleansing. Ignoring his admittedly surprising stamina, you stay under the scalding hot water as long as you possibly can, wishing desperately to be alone by the time you're forced to leave the enclosed sanctity of the shower.

He's there, unfortunately, when you emerge, red and near-raw from the temperature. Your head is swirling, anxiety mixed with steam mixed with too much champagne and too many pills hindering your ability to escape. Todd2 wraps you in some fucking luxurious bathrobe. You hate yourself for collapsing into his arms, and you hate yourself for allowing him to pick you up off of your feet, and you hate him for placing you beside him in the bed you—mercifully and un—fall instantly to sleep in.

CHAPTER TWENTY THREE

Too much.

thoughts for Thots.

You wake up in Todd2's admittedly expensive hotel room.

You wake up hard, head still throbbing violently, instantly aware and afraid that you're not where you should be.

You wake up alone, concerning in its own right, no sign of Todd2 in the bed you must have shared directly after sharing the bed in ways clearly lined out on some contract.

Some contract you feel sick to your stomach about having consummated, stomach following your head in throbbing in some also-concerning rhythm. You're up and escaping to what you pray is the sanctity of an empty bathroom, the only other room in the admittedly expensive hotel room and—by process of elimination—the only other room Todd could be in.

He's not, you discover, discovering some note Todd2 must have left you but bypassing it for the relative sanctity of the toilet you vomit violently into.

Having recovered as much as your violently throbbing head/stomach will allow, you pick up the note and the complimentary bathrobe on your way out of the washroom, settling back onto the bed you had no business sleeping in and discovering via Todd2's admittedly impressive handwriting that the hotel room is yours, and yours alone for the next three hours, checkout time mercifully not until 11 am.

He thanks you eloquently for the night before (again,

mercifully) not specifying specific events or decrying your behavior for specific events, services rendered having exceeded his expectations and reflected on the paper in your trembling, troublingly, hands.

You spend the next two and a half hours unconscious, mercifully adding more sleep to the state of your recovery. You feel like a prostitute, hitting the lobby with your head hung in shame, not willing to provide any checkout verification in the unlikely instance Todd2 hadn't already done so. You noticed he'd hung the Do Not Disturb sign on the outside of the door, begrudgingly impressed with the lengths he'd gone to ensure your comfort. Biggstuddd43 may not have been exactly as advertised—as you breathe fresh air for the first time in far too long, you're thankful your first time providing this horrible/horribly lucrative service was with someone as gentle and as kind as him.

. . .

You go home, and for the first time in months.

You need the kind of soul-cleansing Jessica's penthouse studio/studio apartment can't provide you, its opulence and appointments constant reminder of the debauchery that afforded them.

It feels strange, your place—the key finding resistance from the lock on the front door the way it hadn't previously, as though you've lost the finesse necessary to open a cute one-bedroom apartment door. You've been telling yourself that you're a penthouse suite girl for months now—as the reality of your infinitely smaller living space assaults you with a flick of the light switch, you're instantly brought back to reality.

You find the comfort of your suddenly strange bed and immediately throw yourself into it.

…

Sleep doesn't help.

Not like the pills do—as you wash what you're sure will be the first of today's many with lukewarm tap water, you're grateful to Jessica's seemingly endless array of contacts. (And, in particular, that other plastic surgeon and his liberal use of that little prescription pad.)

You're pretty sure your friends would tell you that you have a problem, if you had friends. As the warmth of the heavy-duty pain medication starts to overwhelm you, you're glad that you don't. The semblance of your conscience is beating you up pretty good all by itself; you don't think you could stand additional admonishings from a Karen or a Becky or a Susan. The whole sex for money thing is an issue, you figure, the way it should be, a far cry from sticking various inanimate objects up your ass for your legion of adoring fans. Who all want to fuck you—the fantasy understood and weaponized into income. The fact that they can fuck you is fucking with you, and in ways you couldn't foresee before the fucking you began.

So you're angry at yourself and not Todd2 for the fucking

and not Jessica for the fucking and the facilitating, sinking into what you assume will be the first of many hot tubs today you're well aware that you've been fucking yourself and over for months and many.

Your new tits float in front of you, a physical reminder of how you've altered yourself in ways you hadn't realized were important to you. The last thought you're able to coherently think—right before you submerge your suddenly weary head under the water—is that maybe the alterations were more important to Jessica.

…

She's called—Jessica—five times.

In the time since the pills took over and before the time the bathwater turned cold, your girlfriend (?) pimp (?) master (?) liberator (?) cared enough to attempt five calls and at least three voicemails. There may be more, but the buzz that has replaced the throbbing tells you that listening to static messages isn't in your best interest just yet. More pills, however, are just what the doctor ordered—after all, you felt the edge wearing off just a little, and you prefer your buzz to be perfectly buzzing.

The bathwater is decidedly stale, and so you meander to the kitchen faucet, bathwater not tenable the way tap water is, facilitating the consumption of the pills you rabidly consume. She calls again, sometime between the uncorking of the bottle of wine you're so relieved to find in the cupboard directly under the kitchen sink and the disappearance of the first half of the bottle. The high is making your fake tits throb—and while you're thankful it's not your head for once, you use it to realize that, for the first time, the newest part of you feels alien.

Foreign, somehow—as though being in this place is physically fucking with you, reminding you of who you used to be. The used to be you couldn't run fast enough away from, sprinting metaphorically in a direction you couldn't realize would end in butt plugs and transactional sex encounters. You vaguely remember a time when TMFWCAT wasn't The Mother Fucker Who Caused All This and just some boy named Esteban/Steve, now simply more catalyst than painful memory. You think about Johnny, the first of many who came after and disappointed you into thinking ThotFineAss420, OnlyFans profile one-million-two-hundred-thousand-forty-three was an identity worth disappearing into. You wanted fake lips and fake tits and a big fake ass and big tattoos, physical manifestation of the emergence of your true, nearly-liberated self. Jessica maybe wanted those things more, liberator/instigator added to the list of increasingly conflicting things you want to call her.

The thought of manipulation leads to thoughts of betrayal; before you know it, you're rationalizing irrational and entirely hypothetical situations, concocting realities from interpretations, and viewing her sexual aggression/dominance in a new, entirely non-theatrical light. She calls as if on queue, number six, and ignored like the previous five, letting the phone vibrate violently on the side of the tub and almost sending it into the water with you while reaching for the wine. You wash down an unhealthy/healthy amount, eyeing the corkscrew you left precariously within reach and allowing your aforementioned rationalization of dark and irrational things to take you to previously unexplored and darker places. You reach for it, scaring yourself with the intent empowering your greedily extended fingers. Opening your wrists, you rationalize irrationally, would be easy, and just maybe offer welcome release from the identity confusion you're experiencing and maybe for the first time.

You're using, and maybe it's to compensate for being used, the post-plastic-surgery pain pills and the booze not half the escape, cumulatively, that arterial bleeds might be. You realize it's cliché, the way your surgically augmented physique is cliché and your descent into prostitution is cliché and your whole life, most likely and upon unnecessary self-reflection, is cliché, and so it takes everything in your admittedly limited power to not close your extended fingers around said corkscrew and kill yourself with it.

...

You don't—kill yourself—and you suppose that's a good thing. You wake up in bathwater that has run itself cold, and you suppose you're shivering. Suppose, because you look like you're vibrating, submerged save for the big fake tits floating out in front of you—but you can't really tell because you still can't really feel. You suppose that is a good thing too, the numb welcome decidedly more than the consciousness. You pull yourself from the freezing water as gingerly as the pills allow, slipping twice and sending water cascading over the tub you're semi-desperately trying to escape. The water welcomes you back, but you're determined, living now somewhat high on the post-pass-out list of priorities you didn't know you had. So you go on—living—your soaked, naked body drip-dripping all over the cute little one-bedroom apartment as you allow your body to tell you that you should probably find something to eat. Sustenance, apparently, is to involve more than pills and wine, and so you take some of the former, washing it down with last sips of the latter, and you go about the business of finding something to eat.

Your empty fridge and barren cupboards indicate that this won't be happening *here*, and so you throw on something you haven't worn in months, marveling at how ill-fitting your new body has altered it into being, and you step into the torturous sun of some mid-day, shambling zombie-like to the sanctity of the coffee shop on the corner.

. . .

You make the mistake of checking your phone in between bites of the bagel that may very well end up being a mistake, too.

You have seventeen missed text messages, and the majority of them are Jessica, and you have thirty-eight missed DM's and the majority of them are horny fans, and you have nine missed OnlyFans notifications, and all of them are horny fans, and you have another twelve emails from prospective Johns on the Sugar Baby dating/prostitution site Jessica maybe bamboozled you into. Of the 76 one-way conversations currently awaiting a response, only two of them seem to give any kind of fuck in regards to how you're doing; Jessica, with her admittedly impressive and seemingly more than surface level of concern as to your whereabouts, and Todd2, with his somewhat sweet lamentations of regret for any negative elements of the experience you experienced the other night.

These stand out, staring back at you from the static on the screen you're staring at, zombie-like, and still undernourished at the coffee shop. You're reading into it, wondering if the feigned interest from Fuckbois and perverts in anything other than seeing the inside of your lady parts is making the level of care from Jessica more than it really is.

You're infatuated with her, or you're in love with her, or you hate her for turning you into the big-tittied, pill-popping prostitute you've become.

...

CHAPTER TWENTY FOUR

Breaking up is hard to do.

thoughts for Thots.

You call her back, Jessica, figuring you at the very least owe it to her to report in. The cynical side of you---the side with the ever-increasing suspicion she's been using you—agrees with the infatuated/in love side's insistence you check-in. So you pick up your phone, and you dial the number you've seen displayed amongst your missed calls bulletins most.

She answers ring-one, and it's

Oh God, I've been so worried about you
and

Where the fuck have you been

and

I've been worried sick

and

I thought you were chained to a radiator in some pervert's third floor fucking apartment

--which is oddly specific, before you can manage a weak

Hello

back.

She says she's worried about you, all

I'm worried about you

and you can tell by the tenor of her voice that she, at the very least, wants you to believe it. She goes on, explaining the lengths she's been going to in order to find you, having tracked down Todd2, and threatened incredibly detailed acts of physical violence upon his person should he be responsible for your admittedly out of character absenteeism. You realize she may be making this more about her and how she feels about your disappearance rather than inquiring as to the why/hows of it, but you're lost in thought, retracing the totality of your time with her and viewing it through the lens of luring/baiting/grooming/deceiving/owning as opposed to loving/sharing/building.

You've got time to because she's going on about what your supposed kidnapping has done to her mental state, proclamations of reports to authorities coming later this afternoon had you not reached out. You question the validity of this, too, reasoning that, although your recorded dalliances are legal, your newly-christened in-person interactions skew dangerously close to prostitution.

Because your newly-christened in-person interactions are prostitution, and so Jessica is lying, at the very least, about the calling the authorities part of her still-ongoing explanations of the lengths she's been going to since you've been gone.

You get a word in, and it's

sorry

and you don't really mean it; forecasting more time away from Jessica might very well be in both your future and best interest. She asks when you're coming home, and the part of you that is unfortunately in love with her recognizes how much it means to hear her call her penthouse studio/studio apartment that particular word; it takes some internal wrangling to substitute

right fucking now

for the infinitely more subdued

soon

you maybe lie when you offer back.

This stops Jessica in her tracks, her previous million-word-per-minute dissertation distilled to dead silence. Your answer—one of any other than the

right fucking now

she was expecting enough to give her pause. It's as though she can sense her previously iron-clad grip on your life slipping; you can't tell if her

just come home

is genuine or genuine as her big fake tits.

Which you miss—along with the rest of her—but you're

remembering that before Jessica, you weren't really into the big fake tits or the women they're attached to, at all.

So her pause gives way to your pause, dead air on the phone where exasperated, one-sided conversation used to be. You tell her that you'll see her soon, hanging up on Jessica before you can decide whether or not you're lying.

...

She's texting you before you get up from the coffee shop table, all

baby, I miss you

at first,

followed by

what about your cam schedule

and the first of the texts that arrive and tell you

it's business

without telling you.

You exit the coffee shop, head hung in contemplation, the realization that home will have to be your cozy little one-bedroom apartment hitting harder than the headache hitting you just after the mid-morning sunlight does.

The pills in your purse tell you to take them; the cloudiness of the Fentanyl or the Hydromorphone or the Oxycodone or the Tramadol or whatever the fuck is in them admittedly welcome release from the mental anguish you're subjecting yourself to.

You don't—take them—walking home and noting the pain increasing with every subsequent step. The physical pain manifestation of—and somehow still dwarfed by— the mental and emotional anguish of your current situation reminds you that self-reflection may be the key to escape.

Escape that is the opposite of the escape the pills offer, and so they stay at the bottom of your purse, your walk home burdened by both the migraine and the emotional trauma that caused it.

CHAPTER TWENTY FIVE

Reve'new'

thoughts for Thots.

You need money.

Not *really*—your last few months of OnlyFans/myfreecams.com/that-one-time-you-were-a-hooker have earned you enough to coast for the next tiny forever, most likely comfortably, but goddamnit, you're a businesswoman. And while the whole sex with relative strangers/addiction to pills has told you that things may have gone too far, you'll be damned if you're going to let one particularly self-destructive bad spell ruin the brand you almost-independently cultivated.

So you spend the next few days sobering up, not taking unnecessary amounts of pain medication, and keeping conversation with Jessica light. Once you've determined that you've regained the lost ability to think somewhat clearly, you pick yourself up off the floor, and you hit the mall.

Hard.

The camera comes first—you do your best to emulate the decidedly sophisticated setup you were becoming far too used to at Jessica's; admittedly, you're a little out of your depth when it comes to understanding the intricacies. So you go for price, reasoning the more expensive apparatus translates directly and understandably to better resolution/quality/whatever. Brad—according to his off-tilt nametag—helps translate the majority of the techno-jargon that comes with shopping in this particular store, and so you're leaving with much more than you'd initially intended, content that your first solo-operated webcam show will go off without a hitch.

(Of course, setting all of this shit up is another story entirely—fortunately, off-tilt nametag Brad was insistent in his offer to come by and set it all up for you, no charge.)

Having tackled the less-fun element of what should be a more-fun/therapeutic endeavor, you hit the first of what will be many kinky little clothing stores, beginning the likely-exhausting search for your new kinky little clothes.

You've got some making up to do, days wrestling with sobriety translating into days without posts or streams translating into days without revenue—revenue the revenue spent on kinky little clothes is sure to translate into more revenue.

So you spend freely, finding that the endorphins the swipe of the credit card generates almost comparable to the endorphins the popping of the pills you used to pop used to generate.

You leave the mall thousands of dollars lighter and dozens of valet-assisted bags heavier; two bags are overflowing with brightly-colored-untastefully-small panties, and two bags are filled with the kind of dresses that would make a stripper blush. Three bags and two boxes are filled with the camera/tech bullshit off-tilt nametag Brad promised to come over and setup and the other four contain some combination of expensive-looking makeup and cheap-looking slutty little outfits and accessories.

The valet piles the bulk of your satisfying little haul into the back of the limo you rented for the day/specifically for this occasion. As you pile in and the driver embarks on the journey back to your cozy little one-bedroom apartment, you're feeling like the worst of the addiction/withdrawal/loneliness might just be behind you.

...

CHAPTER TWENTY SIX

Fun with Insomnia. and pills. and loneliness.

thoughts for Thots.

It's not.

Behind you—you spend the next two nights sleepless. The pills want you to take them, screaming at you from their prison in the bottle in the bottom of the purse you've strewn carelessly by your dresser.

They're relentless, and so you toss and turn just as relentlessly, frustrated by the withdrawals you'd thought you'd overcome and by the all-encompassing insomnia that has followed your forsaking them.

It snuck up on you, this pesky little addiction, intermingled in your addictions to the plastic surgeries that provided them and your addictions to the kinds of things Jessica told you were best for you.

She's telling you, right now, to take the pills screaming at you from their prison in the bottle in the bottom of the purse you've strewn carelessly by your dresser. She's not really, because she's not really here, but you want her to be, the way you want to take the goddamn pills.

The lack of sleep has you hallucinating, and you could use a drink to wash down the pills and the pain the pills promise to numb, missing Jessica and the addictions you're still addicted to, thrashing violently in the bed you're so desperately alone in.

...

The days, mercifully, are better than the nights. You spend the next one, or two, or three fucking around with your new set up—off-tilt nametag Brad had swung by and prepared your new cam room as best he could. Before leaving, he had confessed his love for you, having recognized you at the mall before you'd spent thousands on the equipment he clearly couldn't wait to hook up for you.

He'd left after reminding you—as subtlety as he could—that you hadn't streamed in a "*long-ass time*"—hence the day or two or three preparing for *now*, the moment you're about to make your glorious live return.

You'd been hoping the bags under your admittedly-still-impressive eyes would diminish over time; unmercifully, the sober nights haven't included any rest in them, only violent thrashings and maliciously-intentioned voices.

Voices, like the voices voicing their opinions of your absence across the comments of your various social platforms, encouraging your return with the fervor of the voices in your head at night, encouraging the consumption of narcotics.

You're sober, and you're here, and you're about to stream, sitting in the living room/makeshift studio of your cozy little one-bedroom apartment, wearing something decidedly un-cozy and for the benefit of the thousands about to watch you debase yourself for tips.

You sigh, sign on, hit record, and turn on the first of this evening's many battery-powered dildos, wondering if you sober and in control and in this situation is really you in control at all.

CHAPTER TWENTY SEVEN

Of glorious returns.

thoughts for Thots.

The light blinks red, the way it used to back at Jessica's. Off-tilt nametag Brad told you that when the light blinks red, you're good to go.

You're not—good to go—but you're live, and so you do your best to remove Jessica from your mind, and you do your best to insert the dildo vibrating violently in your hand in somewhere decidedly smaller.

You wince, maybe, and the tips that begin pouring in tells you that wincing is okay and wincing is hot, and the comments that come, comments like

That's hot

tell you that, while you may never be truly separated from your vulnerability, you sure as fuck can weaponize it.

So you push it in a little farther, and the face you make— the face pained by both the violently vibrating dildo in your ass and by the hurt from the people that have hurt/used you translates directly to the surge in tips/cash that makes it all worth it.

There's a sound the tips make when the tips are made, and the speaker from the expensive laptop setup you're setup to is making it, and –from the sounds of it— making it often. Meaning you're making money—as you reach your free hand down the front of your aesthetically pleasing/undulating body, your fingers begin to move in rhythm with the

clink

clink

of the tips you're maybe enjoying making.

It starts to feel good, and so maybe you let your mind drift. Maybe you think about TMFWCAT, and maybe you're all at once thankful for the cheating Esteban /Steve may or may not have done.

Maybe you think about going through that motherfucker's phone, finding what you found, and maybe for the first time, you're entirely thankful you found it.

Your fingers move a little faster; maybe Johnny, the most-significant backup, was really just that and only; a backup, someone to focus your attention on so you weren't focusing your attention on someone else.

Someone like yourself. Fingers moving faster, you're fully focused on you, focusing on the sound of the tips, and the euphoria clarity seems to be bringing. For the first time in forever, the pills don't whisper they miss you, and the booze you preferred to wash them down with doesn't either; you're free to think for yourself here during the cam show you're fucking yourself to. The euphoria builds, and with it, the realization you're emerging from the fire designed to forge you, resplendent in your broadcasted climax with the knowledge that literally thousands are witnessing the release of your inner phoenix.

CHAPTER TWENTY EIGHT

Killin' it.

thoughts for Thots.

You take Jessica to lunch.

Because you can afford it.

Because you're (becoming) rich.

Because it's been a month since you've seen her—a month filled with OnlyFans and cam shows and more. More, like the news you brought Jessica to lunch to share, share because you're hoping she'll be genuinely happy for you, and because you no longer care if she is not.

You don't need her anymore—as she sits at the table across from you, you're not reflecting on times you sat at tables with her to initiate unknowingly arranged sex rendezvous. You're not thinking about the love you thought you felt for her; love maybe better-named admiration if not outright jealousy. You're not thinking about her trendy penthouse studio/studio apartment and how she nursed you back to health after a heavily-influenced series of transformative surgeries. She looks you deep in the eyes, and hers are still fucking seafoam green, and maybe for the first time, it doesn't kill you.

It doesn't kill you because

Jessica has fake hair. (Horse hair extensions.)

Jessica has fake eyelashes. (Mink.)

Jessica has fake cheekbones. (Collagen injections.)

Jessica has a new nose. (Plastic surgery #1.)

Jessica has fake tits. (Plastic surgeries #2 and #3.)

Jessica has had her floating ribs removed.

Jessica has a fake ass.

And so do you—to all or at least most of those things.

And you're younger.

So while it's not a competition, this lunch you're taking Jessica to, it's not-not a competition. And while you're now reasonably sure you're thankful for your time with Jessica and what it has meant to your career (prostitution stint aside), you're now reasonably sure you can stand on your own two (monetized, thanks to your recent discovery of a rather peculiar new fetish) feet.

You exchange pleasantries over sparkling water— sparkling water because being sober means being *sober--* at least for now—and Jessica tells you

she's doing great

but

she misses you

and you tell her

you're doing great

because you are

and

you miss her too

because you do, and because not needing someone doesn't mean you can't miss the good parts about them.

The conversation continues for a while before lunch arrives, and before she asks you about the news that brought you two together, the news you couldn't wait to share in person.

You take a bite of the Ribeye you on your plate, savoring the taste and the look on Jessica's face—the look that says

You don't eat meat

because Jessica had convinced you eating meat wasn't something you do back when listening to Jessica was something you did, too. You allow the moment to linger, linger like the taste of the steak in your mouth, finally washing the taste and the moment down with the wine you sip to deliver the only news that could shock her more than the sight of you eating meat.

So you part your lips, having savored the wine and the moment; part your lips to mouth the words that leave her with the kind of look on her face you kind of came here to see her make.

I'm leaving the cam site

is how you start;

I'm leaving OnlyFans, too

leaving Jessica the kind of in shock you probably would have been yourself a week ago and at the thought of parting your lips to mouth the sounds you just mouthed.

Now—here at the lunch you brought Jessica to in order to proclaim the bold news you've just proclaimed, the euphoria of proclaiming it washes over you.

It's a liberation—the culmination of the tumultuous year you lost yourself in, deconstructed by boys and the acronyms you called them and rebuilt by plastic surgeries and the women and the fans who demanded it. You laid your soul bare and your breasts bare, and you exposed yourself to the world and the adoring fans and the perverts in it. You dabbled in prostitution and pills and languished in self-loathing, all on the way to the email you received last week, the email that reinforced your liberation with a promise (and a contract) that guarantees your days of base defilement are behind you.

The email introduced you to a version of Jessica, resplendent as she is here at the table across from you, who is interested in the kind of partnership that doesn't involve sodomy-by-vibrator; the kind that prefers mutually beneficial monetization via social media...

social media unrestricted by paywalls and restricted by good taste.

She asks what you're talking about, Jessica does, and this time you don't hesitate, parting your lips to tell her

I'm a motherfucking FashionNova partner.

CHAPTER TWENTY NINE

Motherfucking FashionNova.

thoughts for Thots.

You're rich.

The kind of rich that means you'll never have to take your clothes off for money.

Unless you want to.

Which you don't.

You've closed your OnlyFans account, and you've closed your myfreecams.com account, and you're still on Instagram; on Instagram because you're compensated absurdly to be.

Motherfucking FashionNova is paying you to stay clothed; stay clothed in the mountain of free clothes they send you and promise to monthly.

The contract—the contract you signed to represent your escape from sex work—states that you post wearing their clothing and influence your legions of adoring fans to wear it or buy it for their significant others.

Aside from the occasional no-thirstier-than-the-rest-of-them bikini pics, you'll be tastefully clothed in their moderately tasteful clothing, a welcome change from the anal beads and nipple clamps you'd previously endorsed, painfully and without compensation.

Compensation you're receiving, each post representing both their brand and your newfound social media Influencer status. You're happy (relatively), and you're sober (relatively), and you've escaped the trap that pain and pain pills had placed you in.

You're moving out of your cozy little one-bedroom apartment, and you're moving into something relatively more ostentatious and representative of your status and your station and your struggle.

Jessica helps you decorate because Jessica is your friend, now, someone on equal footing and someone you can swap stories with over overly expensive dinners. You tell her about the upcoming fall campaign, and she tells you about the girls she's grooming, and you laugh together over oysters and ordering ridiculously priced living room furniture online.

She keeps you tethered to that world in the only way you'd prefer to be tethered to it, laughing about cam show squirt disasters instead of having them.

She leaves at appropriate times of night, leaving you alone and—for the first time in a few forevers—okay with it, alone in your equally resplendent penthouse studio/studio apartment, sleeping in your California King bed on ten-thousand thread count sheets, and for the totality of the night, unassisted by pills or alcohol.

You're Queen now, rich and fully realized, unbroken on the backs of no-longer-good-enough boys and the games they played to get you here.

He broke up with you, way back when—and you're all the better for it.

BOOK TWO

Her.

thoughts for Thots.

CHAPTER ONE

Her new life is better.

*and other lies she tells herself.
*and me.
*and anyone who will listen.

thoughts for Thots.

She gets off a bus.

Maybe she's from Dakota.

Maybe she's from Vancouver.

Might be West Virginia, might be New Hampshire.

Could be Toronto, could be Dallas.

It might be somewhere pretty; it might be somewhere idyllic. Chances are though, it's somewhere small and small-minded and completely forgettable.

She's here, now.

It doesn't matter why and it doesn't matter where from.

Either-and-any-way-you-slice-it, this bitch is off the bus, moderately-priced footwear landing firmly on Los Angeles concrete.

You have to understand; this is Chapter One because it is a catalyst for the birth of the THOT; the embryo from which a morally carefree, disdainfully liberated butterfly will emerge, beating her proverbial wings (ass cheeks) to the tune of whatever is top of the Hip-Hop charts by the time this book comes out, some six months after it is notorious for being kinda well-written and decidedly more fun.

But back to her.

She's newly reinvented, scantily-clad, and determined to find the next series of what will hopefully turn out to be a better set of circumstances.

She's here—maybe at the behest of a friend who told her she was

too big for her hometown

or

at the behest of every movie she grew up on, particularly the ones about the girls just like her who packed up and came here and *made* it.

She's rented an apartment on a decidedly shitty side of town; away from the bright lights and trendy shops of the side of town she came to take over.

So it's Hollywood, kinda, and she'll settle for an apartment with no furniture of her own on the wrong side of the tracks; for now, her dreams and every movie she's ever seen telling her it's all just a matter of time before she's discovered and her life changes forever.

She pulls the totality of her remaining existence—the suitcase she stuffed everything she could into—from the baggage hold at the front of the bus, and she sets her moderately-priced footwear on the path to the place that will bear witness to her transformation, cliches be damned.

. . .

It sucks, her apartment, the way she thought it would, and more. The advertisement on the internet had claimed it to be 'modestly appointed.' Save the patchwork stained couch and equally suspicious mattress in the corner, 'modestly appointed' means fucking empty.

Her misplaced optimism and giddy enthusiasm overlooks the relative despair of the situation she's moved into, the dream of success foolishly overshadowing the soul-crushing loneliness of boarding a bus in the middle of some likely-Midwestern night only to end up *here*.

She heaves a sigh and places her suitcase in a decidedly unappointed corner of the room, discovering the dilapidated-but-in-a-bohemian/trendy-way bathroom, her reflection in a cracked bathroom mirror reminding her why this trip was worth the soul-crushing attempt.

161

She's stunning—a Midwestern *ten*, the kind of young woman turning heads since young was really a little *too* young. Blissfully unaware that Midwestern ten equals Hollywood six, her perfectly symmetrical features and oddly-colored eyes earned her a degree of laxity with male teachers and a degree of disdain from competing female classmates.

She figures her eyes pop extra violently when contrasted with the dark of her hair, dark like the situation she's found herself in, trapped and not yet aware of it, staring at the resplendent beauty staring back at her from some shitty apartment shitty bathroom mirror.

It's the kind of innocent beauty that makes Hollywood success dreams possible. So she retreats from the flickering light of the bathroom (still) blissfully unaware of the cliches and the pending disappointment lurking in the places the light escapes to, flicking the flickering light off with a brush of the switch and settling into the life she's pretending/praying will be better than the one she's run from.

CHAPTER TWO

She's doing just fine.

thoughts for Thots.

She's not.

And that's okay—after all, she's just escaped to here, leaving one, or two, or three years of her life failing at some post-secondary education program back home—where home was the kind where dreams never really amount to anything.

She's happy, now, waiting tables at some Hipster café before waiting tables at some Hipster bar, her days and nights occupied trying to make the money it will take to pay for the shitty apartment serving as a command center in the war for happiness and fulfillment.

She knows her dreams are the kind that take time in fulfilling—and so menial jobs at borderline-demeaning establishments are to be tolerated if every plotline in every movie she watched to research this dream are to be believed.

So she adjusts the fabric of the too-tight spandex shorts her job description states she wears, and she bends extra low at the tables when delivering drinks to the rich, Hollywood-wannabe douchebags waiting at the tables she waits, confident her fortunes will change soon and enough to justify the change they leave for tips.

So it's onwards and to the next set of circumstances that may (or, to be fair, may not) yield similar/devastating results as the results that resulted in her move here, blissfully unaware that being discovered waiting tables at Hipster cafes and Hipster bars is as unlikely as landing the roles in the auditions she's come here to audition for.

CHAPTER THREE

Darkness at the auditions.

thoughts for Thots.

Mike just wants to see her titties.

The guy beside him, Casting Director Bill, isn't exactly stopping him from asking.

She'd heard that Hollywood had changed, skewing decidedly liberal and a hell of a lot more woke than whatever Red State she'd escaped from...ten minutes into what has already been a nerve-wracking first audition—show-her-titties request notwithstanding—she's learning just how wrong she was.

...

Let's back up a little.

She came here, what was supposed to be a New Hollywood, with the same dreams the girls who came to the Old Hollywood had.

The waiting tables at some Hipster café before waiting tables at some Hipster bar was supposed to lead to discovery by some high-powered New Hollywood executive, and it *did*—but only after months of degrading advances from the kinds of douchebags who prey on the dozens of girls just like her who arrive in New Hollywood seemingly daily.

When it arrived—the genuine discovery by the genuine Hollywood executive—she'd been here long enough to realize just how rare an invitation to audition really was. In the time she'd been waiting tables, literally dozens of similarly starry-eyed girls had come and gone, waiting as they were for the discovery that simply wasn't coming.

It came—her discovery—the month before the last she figured she would spend here, exhausted from waiting tables at some Hipster café before waiting tables at some Hipster bar.

It came in the form of Mike, Mike, the executive from Carolco Pictures. She hadn't yet realized that Carolco Pictures hadn't been in business since 1995—hadn't realized and frankly had been afraid to Google it.

Mike was handsome; in that decidedly sleazy way *all* of the douchebags pretending to be executives were handsome. Mike was just handsome enough and (just a hair) less-sleazy than the rest, just enough and just less than enough to make his particular sleaze tolerable.

So she did—tolerate him—entertaining his pitch and his insistence on buying her a drink after her shift and after said drink insisting she come and meet Casting Director Bill ahead of Casting Director Bill's casting calls for his next film. The film that would undoubtedly launch her career and make her a star.

A star is what she came here to be, and so she accepted his kiss on the cheek and his card, his card with the address to her very first New Hollywood audition.

...

Her audition is now, and

let me see your titties

is a succinct explanation of how it is going.

Under different circumstances, Mike's brand of just-handsome-enough sleaze might result in the honoring of said request.

Here, behind cliché mouth-breathing Casting Director Bill, that request is vehemently denied.

He insists, Mike does, and Casting Director Bill adds something about

never working in this town

and

--amazingly—

something about

going along

and

getting along.

It's as creepy/cliché as it sounds, but the point of Book Two is that creepy/cliché things really do still happen to Thots like her, so it's titties and the reactions their revelation garner that land her this coveted first role, a non-speaking extra is some decidedly-not Carolco

Pictures production of something that is decidedly *not* Hamlet.

With tits.

CHAPTER FOUR

What her search history says about her.

thoughts for Thots.

Nothing good.

Here's some hotness, likely somewhat familiar by now, pulled directly from the same nonsensical should-just-be-inner-monologuing she's feverishly typed into a Google search engine at one time or another:

-what Plastic Surgery will make me hotter

-what Hollywood casting agents are looking for

-Carolco Films (this one is a little late and an unusually worthwhile Google search)

-Mike from Carolco Pictures

-Kylie Jenner lip serum

-Kylie Jenner lip injections

-Kylie Jenner lip injections doctor

-lip injection clinics near me

-breast enhancement surgery cost (duh)

-Brazilian Butt Lift cost

-boobs & ass combo surgery discount

Again, none of this is overly concerning; best believe those of us on the Fuckboi side are still asking equally ridiculous information on our still-overworked search engines.

The concern begins to climb when a pattern emerges—when searches stray from self-improvement surgeries to questions regarding how much porn stars make and if it's more than how much B-movie topless extras make.

Suddenly it's less

-acting classes Hollywood

-affordable acting classes Hollywood

-affordable acting classes in semi-bad near-Hollywood neighborhoods

and more

-how to get into the porn industry

and

-is the casting couch real

and

a whole hell of a lot of what might be a tad unhealthy research.

Still, she's just at the research stage, and the opportunities to audition in an entirely new kind of film remain just that—opportunities. She tells herself there is no such thing as a bad choice when it comes to navigating the avenues that will lead to her eventual superstardom, and so she writes down the names associated with the film companies she may or may not contact, her experience with Mike having proven precedent-setting.

. . .

He helps.

Turns out that—in addition to his somewhat questionable status as Carolco Pictures agent—Mike the executive has contacts in this *other* industry, too.

Casting Director Bill provides insight, also—leaving her detailed voicemails and elaborate text messages outlining the movers and shakers in the industry, admonishing casting directors he doesn't like, and assuring her he'll reach out to those he does.

Mike the executive arranges a series of meetings based on those recommendations, and, before she knows it, research previously reserved for the computer screen is advanced to research in offices with curiously appointed couches.

She's seen enough pornography to realize the casting couch—the

here, have a seat, relax

audition arrangement often turns into somewhat-consensual sex in exchange for film opportunities—but she shows up to the cliché affirming auditions just the same.

Today—Tuesday—marks the first in a series of what Mike assures her will be many—as she settles somewhat on what she hopes will not be a 'traditional' casting couch, she can't help but wonder what awaits her on the other side of the door her interviewer will doubtless emerge from.

CHAPTER FIVE

They're just not that into her, either.

thoughts for Thots.

She's been a bad girl.

They tell her to read it again.

Slower.

Sexier.

She's topless on some horribly cliché casting couch, posing awkwardly/somehow still seductively and arching her back past the point of comfortability. She's slightly defying the laws of physics—if not good taste—lips parted and attempting to please the two sweaty/somewhat menacing men across the room.

The men entered the curiously appointed office some twenty minutes after she arrived, ten minutes late herself, having spent the previous thirty navigating the dimly-lit hallways of the only-somewhat-derelict-looking office building housing their dimly-lit office.

The shorter of the two relatively short men introduced himself as Tomas. He smiled warmly, offsetting a set of peculiarly-set teeth. His unusually long forehead was already home to beads of sweat; as he reached a hand full of disgusting sausage-like fingers to shake hers, she witnessed one errant stream struggling to navigate the creases of his curiously contorted scalp.

This was a welcome distraction from the stares of the taller man; having entered the room directly behind the shuffling of the perspire-r, she felt his gaze both intensely and instantly.

He introduced himself as

Frederick

curtly, offering a distinctly-off-putting limp-wristed handshake before retreating to the opposite end of the curiously appointed room.

As Tomas fought to cut the tension with half-hearted pleasantries, she couldn't happen but notice Frederick's phone escape his pocket and appear at an angle, suggesting he had already begun recording.

Eschewing formality for self-preservation, her eyes left Tomas and his assurances that they represented

the most trusted/accredited production house in the industry

for Frederick and his distinctly odd positioning across the room.

So it's

I've been a bad girl

and

slower

and more suggestively, somehow. She arches her back past the point of reasonable comfort, obliging their subtle suggestions to pinch her nipples and purse her lips.

Tomas assures her this is better for the proverbial camera—and not the camera Frederick may or may not be filming her with on his oddly angled and still-present phone.

After what feels like an absurdly long time contorting topless on what may-or-may-not-be the horribly cliché casting couch, Tomas passively notes that—while her performance was captivating—he feels something is *missing*.

She weighs the also-cliché and ominous tone of his comment against her desire to *make it* in this industry, barely bats an eyelash when Frederick suggests she remove her pants and mount the casting couch, pointing what she hopes is an appropriately amazing ass at the men who insist they hold the key to her career in their sausage finger-laden hands.

. . .

She navigates the maze of dimly-lit hallways some forty-five minutes later, praying her exit from the only-somewhat-derelict-looking office building comes faster than her clearly-lost entrance.

She clutches her purse close to her chest, her undergarments spilling over the side, threatening to fall to the floor as she races towards what she prays is the appropriate exit.

Having finished her meeting well past the point of comfortability, she hadn't bothered to dress fully, collecting the more-complicated of her garments and shoving them into the purse that had somehow been strewn across the floor during the events at the climax of what turned out to be an inherently disastrous encounter.

They hadn't touched her—although, for a moment or two, she was certain she might have to reach for the knife at the bottom of the purse they toppled moving while closer, inspecting the places she now wishes they hadn't. They'd probed her with both questions and intense eye contact, having her repeat

I'm your little slut

while forced to spread her ass on (what she now most certainly understands is) a cliché casting couch.

The assaults weren't physical, but the verbal cut just as deep; she hits the stairs at the end of the hall hard, remembering their claims that she wasn't slutty enough or young enough to fill the kinds of roles they were aiming to fill.

They called her

Midwestern plain

and

lacking in the emotive qualities necessary to lend credibility

--whatever the fuck that means

in and amongst the myriad of other reasons they discounted her, not even waiting for her to cover the more private of her exposed parts before thanking her for her time and exiting the confines of the interview room.

She reaches the sidewalk just as the sun sets behind the towering buildings on the horizon; the nice part of town seeming impossibly far away and the metaphor of fading light not lost on her as she waits for the Uber to take her to the home she realizes is anything but.

CHAPTER SIX

She was never really there.

thoughts for Thots.

Sometime between leaving her casting couch audition and returning to the sobering reality of her apartment on the wrong side of town, she's going to have to answer some questions.

Questions about the reality of her chosen reality—whether or not the commitment to the dream and the ensuing move out here was worth the constant toplessness and the constant disappointment.

Whether or not waiting tables at some Hipster café before waiting tables at some Hipster bar is going to lead to the discovery that maybe should have happened by now; happened and happened maybe more than auditions requiring constant toplessness.

She realizes she's one of many who moved out with the same dream only to move back; of those still here, she reckons it's important to count herself among those who haven't given up.

So she waits and for a call that maybe never come, waiting tables before waiting tables and waiting, desperately, for the call that could change her life.

The weeks pass mercilessly; every moment spent waiting for the feedback from her audition or confirmation of the next. Mike, the executive from Carolco Films, checks in, but she's relatively sure Mike checks in because Mike foolishly believes she'll sleep with him.

She's overworked and underestimated and horribly under-slept—the tips coming from waiting tables doing little to offset the costs of living here, the place she's now painfully aware that dreams come to die.

And hers most assuredly *is*—with no friends to speak of and no furniture to speak of, she's finding it increasingly difficult to remain tethered to the idea that the call is coming—the call that will tell her she's the next (adult) film star, the call that will save her proverbial existence.

She considers running away from the nowhere-near-finished one year lease on her nowhere-near-furnished apartment; turning/tucking tail and heading home,

Dakota

or

Vancouver

or

West Virginia or New Hampshire or Toronto or Dallas home and decidedly more so than Hollywood.

She's debating the merits of the call to the parents she ran from, weathering their admonishings in exchange for the possibility of refuge, wondering for how long she'll be forced to endure tersely worded

I told you so-s

before settling back into the kind of life they'd told her she would always have.

She tells herself Wednesday will be the day, the day she makes the decision, and the day because today is Thursday and Thursday is about as far away from Wednesday as one can comfortably be.

…

It's Tuesday night before the phone rings.

It rings late—late enough to interrupt the sleep she's just fallen into; the kind of sleep that's overly necessary and under-realized—the kind that had just come after a week of stress and serving tables.

So her

hello

has some *rasp* to it, coming off as unenthused to be awake and answering as she most certainly is.

She realizes—moments later and reinforced by the opposite amount of enthusiasm on the other end—that the rasp in her voice may very likely save her life.

Yessss

the voice on the other end of the phone affirms with absolutely no context

jut like that !!

She's confused and annoyed and more than ready to hang up and attempt to recapture the sleep that has just escaped her when the voice on the other end of the phone proclaims

You're perfect for my film

and, just like that, the night before she gives up and moves home becomes the night before she becomes the second lead in Frederick and Tomas' production of

I've Been A Bad Girl 4.

CHAPTER SEVEN

Sad puss, on film.

thoughts for Thots.

She fucked him.

On film, which is kind of the point, pornography like the one she's just filmed

I've Been A Bad Girl 4

dictating that her 'acting career' involves a little bit of acting and more sex with strangers.

He said his real name is Marcus. She appreciated that— *Rod Hardson* a decidedly disingenuous call sheet/stage name, appearing cold and alien the first time she read the scene description and the description of her impossibly well-endowed co-star.

The scene called for the type of thing she imagined all of these scenes call for; a chance sexual encounter with an impossibly well-endowed dishwasher repairman, when all she really called for was a dishwasher repair.

She tells herself she acted surprised when Rod Hardson knocked on the door to her soundstage/fake-apartment—after all, the scene called for it.

She tells herself she conveyed the script's emotion brilliantly, the coquettish grin, the reservations when bartering over price, the mock/not mock horror when Rod Hardson whipped out his angry erect penis and demanded compensation for services rendered.

The Uber home is filled with reflections like those—the hours of well-lit carnality that followed, the multiple takes, and the outright anxiety before, during and after the mock/not mock aggressive sex decidedly not worth the reflection her emerging thespian prowess is.

After all, she's an actress

Goddess

if Frederick's elated producer-chair comments are to be believed. His assurances that her performance is set to eclipse that of

I've Been A Bad Girl

series lead Roxanne Von Slut's recent output empowers her the totality of the drive home. And the duration of the hot shower that follows, rinsing away the sins of the day before indulging in a bottle of wine and the ordering of the pizza the wine encourages, her mind racing at the possibilities her star-making turn is sure to afford.

Day Two of filming turns out much the same; she learns about blocking and lighting and editing and—uncomfortably—re-shooting, which, Frederick assures her, is something of a rarity.

Her performance, he claims, was so transformative, so enthralling, that her (unnamed) character demanded a follow-up scene. Apparently, Rod Hardson had raved about her the previous day, insisting she had been a natural and that his slotted scene with the perky blonde be substituted for another scene with perky *her*.

She was flattered to hear it and flattered to be invited back and today—Day Two—ends with the same elated-if-somewhat-sore Uber ride home. What was originally intended to be a second-billing on a one-day shoot has turned into an elaborate two-scene, three-day production—a rarity in the porn world, if Frederick and Tomas are to be believed.

So it's home and another, larger bottle of wine and (don't tell anyone) pizza for dinner again and the kind of sleep that comes with the satisfaction of hard work accomplished--the only work remaining picking an appropriately suitable stage name of her own.

Day Three, and Rod Hardson is

big

and

black

and

back

and,

according to Frederick, right under that proclamation on the front of the DVD/digital release cover, her as-of-yet-undecided-upon stage name will now sit, sit, and higher than the perky blonde she was to play second fiddle to just two days ago.

And all she has to do to secure her spot is have sex with a man on film for the third consecutive day in a row. Although her aching body reminds her that this is not as easy as it sounds, she takes it in the kind of stride she imagines the stars do, moaning and arching as theatrically as a top-billed porno star *should*.

Rod Hardson finishes, mercifully, some twenty-minutes later; she finds her feet, imagines herself shaking like Bambi on the ice in that Bambi movie she saw back home, and absorbs Frederick and Tomas' adulations and assurances that this is the beginning of something big.

Big

like Rod Hardson, who offers her a warm, soft terrycloth robe, with the word 'star' emblazoned on the back, and after draping the robe over her still-shaking body offers her a warm Rod Hardson smile and then offers her a warm invitation to dinner, tonight.

So Day Three wraps the best of all three and

I've Been A Bad Girl 4

wraps production right around the time she realizes her thoughts of giving up and going home are a wrap, too.

CHAPTER EIGHT

He's different, too.

thoughts for Thots.

She doesn't need a man to validate her.

She doesn't need to be in a relationship—or some semblance of a relationship—to feel beautiful or wanted or complete.

But it sure fucking helps.

It's been a month since the momentous filming of her forthcoming feature film debut, and while the dividends from

I've Been A Bad Girl 4

have yet to come in, the dividends of filming

I've Been A Bad Girl 4

with Rod Hardson most certainly have.

In the month since he took her on that first dinner date—to some so-trendy-she-couldn't-pronounce-the-name Hollywood hotspot, she's spent almost every night since on dinner dates or similarly exciting adventures with Marcus.

Rod Hardson, on film and in the bedroom (and the kitchen, and the park, and the every-inch-of-his-admittedly-well-appointed-and-suitably-huge-apartment) is *just* Marcus now, Marcus the man she's been spending every night adventuring with.

So she's a star (or soon to be), and she's no longer alone, and she's no longer contemplating leaving this wonderful life she's spent the last month relishing.

And all it took to get here was three consecutive days of animalistic sex on camera.

All it will take to stay here, she assures herself, will be to continue to navigate the morally murky waters of the adult film industry, aligning herself with the *lesser* of the totally creepy adult entertainment producers. That—combined with all kinds of beneficial alliances with men like Marcus—have turned what was initially an admittedly doomed tenure in Hollywood to a particularly thriving one.

Tonight, like most, they're seated in the center of some bougie Hollywood hotspot, sucking back oysters and celebrating the still-can-go-places anonymity that comes with relative newcomers in a town desperate to—but as of yet unsuccessful at—uncovering them.

The same can't be said for the pop star some four tables over; she looks to be having a decidedly *worse* evening, having been hounded by the paparazzi stationed curbside before sitting at the table she sits at, hounded now by her fellow patrons for photographs and autographs and other flattering annoyances.

She remembers asking Marcus weeks ago—when the phenomenon of being in an establishment with even 'c-level' celebrities first dawned upon her—why, despite Rod Hardson's prolific presence in the adult entertainment industry, he wasn't similarly swarmed.

He informed her—with one of the similarly disarming smiles he happens to be smiling at her right now—that the men in porn amount to so much as window dressing; they're *there*, but compared to the female stars of the films he stars in, they're not really there at all.

So it's dinners like dinner tonight, shucking oysters and rubbing elbows with the rich and the glamorous and for the duration of the time until the time comes that she's famous and celebrated for the choices she made to stay here.

Although she came here with the misguided enthusiasm so many young men and women do—the assumption that traditional Hollywood success was the ultimate goal—she realizes that the success of the porno star or the social media Influencer might be even more ideal. All of the money and the freedom money brings, and less of the cages—the paparazzi and the inability to go anywhere and the constant and crushing scrutiny.

If she's a bastion of what she's calling *Nu-Hollywood*—the trappings of fame bestowed upon one without the *trappings* of fame—she's entirely satisfied with how this particular journey has turned out.

CHAPTER NINE

Fuckbois still suck.

thoughts for Thots.

They really do.

Adult-film-Fuckbois suck the most.

They're handsome/beautiful, which is how they get away with it, and horny, which is why they can't go five days without acting in adult films or booking their next one.

Marcus warned her about their kind, assuring her with honeyed words and copious amounts of time together that he was different.

She believed him wholeheartedly if wondering somewhat as to the extent of his exaggerations. Now, on set for the day's shooting of her second video, she realizes just how right he was.

…

Her first scene hit Pornhub two months ago.

The time since has been strange.

Within hours her video debut was trending, hundreds of thousands of views accumulated overnight. Tomas and Frederick assure her that the physical copies—turns out they are still a thing—of *I've Been A Bad Girl 4* are doing exceptionally well also.

They must have realized she was something of a commodity; in the time since her scenes hit the adult pornography websites, Tomas and Frederick have called at least three times per day, offering work with the upper-tier pornographers shooting in Hollywood. She'd declined four offers before accepting *this* one, a shoot at a rented mansion in the Hollywood Hills, glamorous and extravagant and near-perfect.

Near perfect, thanks (in part) to her co-star, a well renowned/unfortunately-also-well-endowed/entitled douchebag dubbed Hollywood Rick.

...

Hollywood Rick is yelling at her right now, leaning menacingly over the clearly-not-equipped-to-handle-him director, having seen the playback on the latest scene and apparently been left unsatisfied.

In the half-day she's spent on set, Hollywood Rick has displayed similarly petulant behavior a half-dozen times. Although she'd tuned him out after the first three outbursts, she's reasonably sure this is the first time she's been the target of his wrath.

He's displeased, apparently, with her level of enthusiasm during the scene they've just completed...the scene involving a ridiculous amount of baby oil and a decidedly too-expensive-to-be-covered-in-baby-oil Restoration Hardware sofa.

From what she can discern—navigating the onslaught of

fucking useless

amateur

self-indulgent

cunt

's he's continually peppering his diatribe with; her Tomas-and-Frederick-pleasing facial impressions have taken away from the nuances of his performance.

This—judging by the trajectory of the banana he's launched somewhat effeminately from the craft services table in her general direction—is an affront that isn't to be tolerated.

From her vantage point, on the other side of the admittedly cavernous Hollywood Hills mansion-sized living room, well out of danger from his limp-wristed banana tossing wrath, Hollywood Rick appears to be breaking out in hives, his rage reacting poorly with the baby oil she's also covered in.

This, unfortunately for everyone within auditory range, is pointed out to him by a cowering production aid and results in the flipping of the modestly appointed craft services table.

Questionably dressed sandwiches rain down on questionably dressed talent as producers, gaffers, and terrified onlookers scatter. Hollywood Rick—having seen his bizarrely red visage in an impressively expensive floor-to-ceiling Hollywood Hills mansion mirror—

continues his rage unabated, picking up an equally-expensive looking camera and threatening to smash it before Frederick and Tomas attempt to ensnare his outstretched and flailing arms.

This—as a result of both his petulant thrashings and the copious amounts of oil adorning his forearms—results in the immediate dropping of the expensive-looking camera.

Which results in the immediate ending of the day's shoot.

Which results in the immediate ending of any hopes to reshoot the day's scene—the day's scene she was apparently enjoying the fake/not fake sex a little *too* much in.

Which results in the immediate understanding that Adult-film-Fuckbois really do suck the most.

CHAPTER TEN

Still creepin'.

thoughts for Thots.

Her Hollywood Rick induced sex sabbatical doesn't last.

She's back on set the very next day, the rental of the Hollywood Hills mansion apparently informing the decision to get right back to it.

Hollywood Rick has been replaced, mercifully, by Marcus—turns out Rod Hardson took a break from grocery shopping Sunday to fill a series of holes in the shooting schedule.

Including *hers*, one of three and one of three girls her man has been tasked with pleasing in order to fill the scene checklist Tomas and Frederick so desperately need filling.

He had asked her—the night before and only after expressing his sympathies for the events of the day when she told him—if she would be jealous of his proposed three-girl-filling filling in.

She'd found it sweet, his earnestness, compounded no doubt by the contrasting behavior of the *other* adult entertainer she'd interacted with that day and assured him that—despite the pleasant trajectory of their budding relationship—she understood completely his professional obligation to please women comma *plenty*.

He was, after all, Rod Hardson—as she reminded him, recounting the events of the day, he had to represent similarly well-endowed, non-petulant male entertainers, lest the weekend's disaster reach the ears of other porn producers.

She did notice, however, his utter contempt for Hollywood Rick—who, up until the events of yesterday and the murder of the craft services table—had been at least a work acquaintance, if not a friend.

She chalks it up to an affront on the professionalism of his chosen trade, hoping his vitriol for Hollywood Rick has nothing to do with the fact that he and his unfortunately also-well-endowed-male-pornstar ass ended up deep inside of hers.

She may be relatively brand new to the adult entertainment industry, but she's hyper-aware that there is no room for jealousy within it.

So she's back on set, Sunday, and after Marcus—Rod Hardson—completes his vigorous role in the reshooting of yesterday's unusable scene, she opts out of today's attempt at a less messy craft services table and watches his impressive/equally as vigorous takedown of her three equally beautiful co-stars, blissfully not jealous and ignoring the sinking suspicion gnawing at the back of her mind that the feeling may not be reciprocated.

She's completely enthralled by the pounding he's giving sweet little Tiffany, happy and satisfied and convinced the day will end without the drama of the previous—

--when a shattering of the glass of a nearby window reminds her that her new life is nothing like her old one.

CHAPTER ELEVEN

The ballad of Hollywood Rick.

thoughts for Thots.

She's not okay.

She's really not.

Moments ago, Hollywood Rick threw a piece of undoubtedly expensive patio furniture through one of the floor to ceiling glass windows separating the pornographic film filming indoors from outside, and the storm Hollywood Rick was apparently outside raging in.

Cocaine, she reasons, is a hell of a drug and the reason—or at least a sizeable part of the reason—Hollywood Rick is tackling Tomas in a corner of the now-raining-indoors rented Hollywood Hills mansion he's doing his best to ruin.

And the shoot certainly is—ruined—as the poor craft services table buckles under the weight of Hollywood Rick's rage and subsequent tackling of Tomas atop it.

The living room is a mess of glass and rain and finger foods and big-fake-tittied topless girls. The storm is inside now, literally and metaphorically, as Tomas writhes under Hollywood Rick's somehow still oiled body, screaming as enthusiastically as the loudest of the big-fake-tittied topless girls headed for non-shattered living room furniture to duck under.

A quick glance around the living room uncovers more than big-fake-tittied topless girls under cover of post-modern furnishings; Frederick appears to be filming, slack-jawed and yet seemingly unconcerned with the plight of his minuscule producer/partner.

Rod Hardson, having witnessed the assault from across the not-unrealistic-to-say football-field-sized living room, has left the sanctity of Michelle's anus. Switching deftly from filmed adult entertainment actor to filmed action movie actor, he's sprinting as enthusiastically as he was just fucking and towards the calamity unfolding underneath the remains of the not-supposed-to-fold-that-way craft services table.

She recognizes the inclination to scream—to join the cacophony of shrill voices raining like the rain when it shouldn't be/inside the rented/ruined Hollywood Hills mansion—but she catches herself, instead watching silently as Marcus tackles Hollywood Rick.

Tomas, liberated by the tackling and the ensuing rolling Hollywood Rick is rolling and away from him, screams as shrilly as the big-fake-tittied topless girls he's been screaming in tandem with, screams orders of stopping and among the kinds of curse words that could make the big-fake-tittied topless girls stop screaming, could they hear him over their own.

Marcus and Hollywood Rick don't—stop—rolling around football-field-sized living room floors, trading punches and profanity-filled insults amongst torrents of rain and smatterings of shattered glass.

She's amazed, somewhat, at the relative calm she's surveying the scene with—calm, relative to the din the combined screams are making all around her, as Marcus appears to be getting the better of a now-also-screaming Hollywood Rick.

She's aware that she's not screaming, denying a still-present inclination as Hollywood Rick grabs the man dubbed Rod Hardson—her man—by the balls—her balls—and proceeds to attempt to crush them in his somehow still-oiled palm.

Recognizing the cowardice in his attack, she moves to intercept them, rolling as they are and towards her. Tomas and a random big-fake-tittied-topless girl run past her on her way to them, the shrill of their combined screams almost enough to deter her from her course.

But Rod Hardson is screaming too, caught off guard by Hollywood Rick's schoolyard bully tactics. Deciding discretion is the better part of valor, she grabs a carelessly strewn 12-inch strap on dildo from beside the overturned craft services table and proceeds to beat Hollywood Rick across the forehead with it.

Now *he* screams, Hollywood Rick, and louder than her man, releasing his balls from a somehow-still-oiled grasp as he proceeds to curl into something resembling a fetal position beneath her.

She strikes him again, furious at both the indignation he has caused the shoot and her weekend and—least of all—her man. Somewhere behind her, Tomas shrieks in unadulterated glee as Frederick continues filming the chaos. Somewhere between strike four and strike seven

Marcus regains his feet, somewhat still doubled in agony as he joins her in beating the writhing, somehow-still-oiled, now-sobbing body beneath them.

So she's still not okay

but her weekend ends on a somewhat satisfactory note, revenge on the revenge-intended Hollywood Rick and—unbeknownst to her—the breakthrough star of a new type of reality TV themed porno.

It's not until the following Tuesday—following Frederick's cocaine-powered Zoom call—she learns that what began as a relatively routine shoot has birthed—lawsuits pending—*Porn Stars Gone Wild Episode 1: The Emasculation of Hollywood Rick*.

CHAPTER TWELVE

Her new man is jealous.

*and other potentially problematic concerns.

*and stuff about porn.

thoughts for Thots.

Ugh.

He's jealous.

Where is this coming from?

Because it certainly is unbecoming of him.

It's been two months since The Hollywood Rick Incident; six weeks since The Hollywood Rick Incident made its way onto Pornhub.

In the six weeks since, *Porn Stars Gone Wild Episode 1: The Emasculation of Hollywood Rick* has been trending on Twitter, top of numerous porn search engine queries, and the topic of porn-related podcasts she quite frankly didn't know existed.

Like this one, the one she's on right now and can't quite remember the name of, sitting across from some overly enthusiastic hosts/fans and recounting—for what feels like the sixtieth time in six weeks—the events of the weekend that spawned her porn-pop-culture takeover.

Marcus sits silently beside her, guest number two and the recipient of zero questions and decidedly more scorn, the hosts of this not-remembered/unnamed podcast referring to him only in the description of a man saved by a 12-inch strap-on dildo wielding super-heroine.

By the time they get to asking "smash or pass" regarding her fellow sex-industry personalities—a series of screenshots of porn stars followed by questions of whether or not she'd fuck them—Marcus is exiting the studio, at least unceremoniously enough to elicit an on-air reaction from the gossip-farming hosts.

She finishes the rest of the awkward interview alone, somewhat distracted by his latest micro-aggression, freshest in a series of increasingly less passive attempts to show her he's uneasy with her newfound fame.

Six weeks of increasingly less-quiet escalations have led them here, specifically, her leaving the podcast studio alone and calling an Uber home and wondering the duration of the drive if her man will be at their now-shared home when she arrives.

...

She does—arrive—mind already good and distracted from the script for tomorrow's scene she should be focusing on—'reality' porn about as real as 'reality' TV, so not really real at all.

As the star of Frederick and Tomas' emerging blockbuster pornographic film franchise, her commitment to professionalism demands that—aside from appearing on a steadily-increasing array of interview platforms—she spends her nights studying lines and going over scene outlines, not fighting with well-endowed confidence-lacking co-stars/boyfriends.

She finds him on the couch. Somewhat relieved not to have to search the entirety of his/their-now-shared compound for him, she gives herself a moment to hang her coat, put away her purse before joining him, a signal that the evening fight is now free to begin.

He's not the yelling type, so the argument begins on the decidedly passive end of the passive/aggressive spectrum; his casual

How did the interview go

coming off equal parts feigned interest and convenient exclusion of the fact he was there for most of it.

He sits, eyes forward, and trained upon the ludicrously large flat screen mounted on the wall across their shared living room.

Unflinching, he thumbs aimlessly at the increasingly omnipresent video game controller in his hands, altogether less interested in her

They nominated me for some end-of-year award

than the latest killstreak/whatever-the-fuck that is he's spent the better part of the past six weeks obsessing over.

She repeats herself, foolishly hoping that he'd simply not heard her before,

They nominated me for some end-of-year award

falling on the same deaf ears as the previous attempt.

So it's

What the fuck is your problem

instead, favoring the aggressive end of the passive/aggressive spectrum, remembering the need to go over scene outlines for tomorrow's sheet.

He bites, thumbing the pause button, indicating with a sigh and a turn of the head that her question is worth the momentary killstreak seeking reprieve she was looking for.

No problem

he lies in response, his beautiful and-not-just-in-a-pornstar-way features seemingly more chiseled under the soft living room light.

Which makes battling him more frustrating somehow, the inconsistencies in his behavior over the past month and a half compounded when measured against the fact she'd rather just *not*.

Battle him,

but her jaw is set as firmly and almost-as-impressively as his, and so it's

Are you jealous?

and

because you're being a fucking asshole

and

as incendiary as it sounds.

He sighs again, her aggression enough to warrant the placement of the lately-omnipresent video game controller upon the surface of the expensive glass table they'd recently invested in, a measured

I've seen this before

as curt and matter-of-fact as it sounds.

Still heated, she goes with a shaking of her head and a flailing of her arms, indicating as violently/non-verbally as she can that

    a)   she has no idea what he's talking about

and

    b)   he's avoiding the undeniable fact that this fight is directly related to the podcast he stormed out of and the underlying reasons why.

His lack of escalation serves to both infuriate her and cause her to escalate more; her observations as to his behaviors come more vividly now, and with a deterioration in the eloquence of her chosen phrasings.

He simply sighs, watches her with those dead-set, frustratingly beautiful features, and waits for her to exhaust herself in the damning of his recent behaviors.

Sensing the irony in the situation, and beyond frustrated, she folds herself onto the couch beside him, fully aware that—in her overly descriptive accusations, she's become less the victim and more the villain—despite his wordless vacancy at the studio just hours before.

Contrasted with his rolling-around-mansion-living-room-floor fights just two months before, his lack of passionate engagement in fights *non*-physical has left her as exhausted as trying to determine the reasons for his declining enthusiasm at her newfound porn ascendency.

So it's *less* about

end of year award nominations

and it's less about

what the fuck is your problem

and more about

What's the matter

and

You've seen what before

spoken decidedly more softly than the previous approach.

Apparently, this approach is more pleasing—the video game controller remains on the coffee table and the frustratingly beautiful features soften, and he spends the better part of the next hour detailing the plight of ascending porn stars just like her.

CHAPTER THIRTEEN

OnlyFans.

*and the subsequent death of traditional porn.

thoughts for Thots.

Marcus says he's seen it before.

More than once.

More than twice, even.

Young girl from some small town somewhere comes *here*, this cesspool of sin and vice, Iseeking some glamour that exists only when radiated illusion-like from the screen on the TV she used to watch back home.

They go to auditions, fail, and then go to auditions of a different kind, auditioning for producers like Frederick and Tomas—producers who, Marcus assures, are decidedly better than the multitude of third-rate pornographers/pimps running the scum-filled industry girls just like her end up auditioning to be a part of.

Invariably, he assures, they find some measure of success, ascendancies being both relative to and relegated to the industry they decidedly-did-not get on a bus or a train or a plane to be a part of.

Marcus says he's seen it before

More than once

More than twice, even

where they let it go to their heads *anyways*, all of a sudden big fish in the small cesspool that is the industry he too is admittedly a part of.

It's different for girls, he assures her, different for girls like her who develop a false sense of importance relative to their positioning in a male-dominated hierarchy. Marcus assures her that she is only as good in value as the voracity of her last scene—that, coupled with the still-relative anonymity of her contrasted to the online catalog of her predecessors/now peers adding to the fantasy in her audience that the scenes—despite cringe-inducing titles like *Pornstars Gone Wild*—are *not*-scripted acts of depravity that just happened to be caught on film *and* ruthlessly edited *and* distributed for mass consumption.

He tells her that—following the next scene or the next scene—she'll lose the sense of ambiguity that has helped her ascendency, the luster worn off her shocking emergence, and that—with offers for subsequent scenes dwindling as fast as they'd appeared only weeks before—she'll be encouraged to participate in a series of shocking escalations in order to attempt to recapture the interest of fickle producers and fickle, insatiable-for-the-*next*-her fans.

So it's two fingers in the ass, or mild-electrocution, or a gangbang of piss-on-her-not-nearly-as-talented-or-delicate male performers to service at once and on camera and for a fraction of the fees she'd commanded just two fingers ago.

He tells her he's seen it before

More than once

etc.

And suddenly, what appeared to be jealousy at her no-longer-unique sounding ascendency is cast in an entirely new, not-nearly-as-jealous-sounding light.

Marcus tells her this, and—for the first time in the admittedly delirious blur that has been the past eight weeks—she's viewing the industry she's somehow fallen into with the revulsion associated more with the version of her that left that initial casting couch audition.

She feels used, and she feels unanchored and—curled up attentively on the couch the way she has been for the better part of the last hour listening to Marcus and his mesmerizing illuminations—she feels entirely too sober to think about reading lines or scenes for tomorrow, much less getting fucked in them.

He reads the room, she figures, recognizing most likely by her rapt engagement that the fire in any previously-planned rebuttal has gone out; stopping only to take an exaggerated breath, he continues describing the horrors he's witnessed over the years he's been an active participant in the industry he's damning.

He says he's doing this because he cares about her, cares about her in a way he maybe didn't care about the ones he's seen fall victim to the apparent horrors of porn before. He keeps her invested and silent during the remainder of his verbal dissertation, hammering home a series of points that destroy her assumptions that his behaviors over the past six weeks, before unexpectedly evolving the dialogue into something she doesn't see coming—

--a solution.

OnlyFans.

She feels her cheeks blushing, admittedly embarrassed and ignorant and overwhelmed, feeling very much like the foolish girl who stepped off of a bus just months before. She's embarrassed to admit that—despite what she would call a comparatively healthy Instagram following, she's decidedly unaware of OnlyFans.

He enlightens her, reaching for his phone and opening his browser, all the while praising the platform and going so far as to call it

the death of traditional porn.

He says he'd considered an account himself, but that male Influencers, actors, and adult industry entertainers make a fraction of what popular females do.

He turns his phone to her, allows her to take it in her hands. (As relatively ignorant as she sometimes feels, she's savvy enough to realize him granting her access to his phone—including what appears to be a healthy level of subscriptions to this platform—is a very big deal.)

He calls his level of engagement with OnlyFans

'important' and she believes him—believes him because the past six weeks of increasingly not believing him have been exhausting and believes him because his breakdown of her newfound profession has left her incredibly receptive to his proposed solution.

He tells her that content creators receive payment directly from followers in two ways—tips and subscriptions—subscriptions, which, as she determines thumbing through the few he subscribes to—earn creators anywhere from five to thirty-five dollars per month.

Per subscriber

he excitedly explains

and some girls have thousands of 'em.

She's scrolling excitedly, witness to acts of various sexual degradation and tasteful nudity and not-so-tasteful nudity and some—to her surprise—with relatively no nudity at all.

He claims that the bigger the entertainer's platform—the greater the following, the higher the awareness—the greater the earning potential. She verifies this, noting some social media personalities and even a semi-famous singer amongst the accounts he pays a monthly subscription fee to—her line of questioning upon discovering his hundred-plus dollar a month vice is *less* jealous girlfriend and *more* intrigued potential participant.

So the fight has left her, replaced by an interest in abandoning the industry that has just gained her a modicum of fame in favor of an industry designed to capitalize/monetize said fame upon the dollars of the individuals who built it. She figures he knows better, Marcus, about the pitfalls of an industry she hasn't really experienced yet—violence from Hollywood Rick aside—and that taking his advice and moving her career to the business owner phase is a logical progression for the type of Independent Woman she's only now realizing she wants to be. Unless she's a producer, traditional porn no longer makes sense.

The remainder of the night isn't spent arguing with Marcus or going over scene outlines and studying lines— aside from a quick

I quit

voicemail on Frederick's phone, the majority of her night is spent launching her very own OnlyFans page.

CHAPTER FOURTEEN

Her OnlyFans.

thoughts for Thots.

Her new day job—aside from taking naked pictures of herself and avoiding calls from a surely-exacerbated Frederick and Tomas—is liking pictures of other Instagram Thots who have taken naked pictures of themselves.

Marcus assures her that this is the path to increased revenue; that her own Instagram (linked, of course, to her budding OnlyFans via a clever *click the link to see completely uncensored pics and videos kiss emoji kiss emoji squirt emoji*) will grow directly as a result of her increased interaction with similar Influencers.

A week passes—a week that would have otherwise been spent having sex in a series of uncomfortable positions observed by an uncomfortable amount of unfortunate-looking onlookers/filmers/co-stars—and Marcus and his insight into the burgeoning future of adult entertainment proves accurate—her Instagram audience grows exponentially, now filled with the only-slightly-more-tame type of content

completely uncensored

on her OnlyFans.

The week sees Marcus shoot the majority of her content—a welcome, loving, supportive far cry from (Frederick and Tomas aside) the types of callous, rude photographers/filmers she surely would have been exposed to with increased exposure to the traditional porn scene.

He even appears in some—porn scenes she's filming (in preparation for next week's graduation from uncensored pics and masturbation videos to full-on sex--) dusting off the Rod Hardson persona in order to bring his audience to her page as well.

She feels a *little* bad for quitting over voicemail and ignoring their quite-frankly-flattering frequent/near-constant attempts to coerce her back to porn, but the steady increase in her subscriber base

Only $19.95 per month

goes a long way to reassuring her that the decision was a good one. As Marcus reminds her (and only in moments of weakness, usually covered in baby oil and assaulted by a series of clickings from newly-purchased cameras), she's capitalizing on an audience she'd earned from *Pornstars Gone Wild* without losing a terrible percentage of profits paying producers, directors, co-stars and rented mansion/rented mansion repair costs.

Once that first weekly (rolling—so by the 8th of the month she should have her payment from the creation of her page, conveniently on the first of the month) payment comes through, he promises, any lingering thoughts of betrayal or abandonment or misplaced loyalty will be replaced with thoughts of which real estate development to invest in and how many Louboutins to buy and whether she wants the Porsche or the Land Rover or *both*.

It makes content creation easier, and it makes content creation fun. The only foreign objects inside of her are foreign objects she chooses; foreign and in places teased appropriately on Instagram with links *in* and *to* places said placings pay off.

The way they *are*, her audiences growing, and her enthusiasm at perhaps the highest since she bought the ticket for that bus all of those months ago.

She thanks Marcus for his support and his encouragement (and his occasional participation) with gifts paid for in advance of her first real paycheque. The numbers projected for the end of her first paid week are making the decision comfortable and reassuring her that she can certainly fucking afford it.

CHAPTER FIFTEEN

Collabs.

*of a different kind, with the same person from Book One.

thoughts for Thots.

Jessica is mid-tier Instagram famous, and Jessica has an OnlyFans with hundreds of subscribers, and, in person, Jessica is stunningly beautiful.

Marcus, having known her from both his Rod Hardson days of fucking everyone even remotely associated with the porn industry and having known her from being a subscriber to her page since Day One, had arranged a meeting *here*, some trendy café she's meeting her at.

She assumes Jessica agreed to the meeting because—according to Instagram and OnlyFans—she's one of the hottest up and coming Influencers on the local scene.

This meeting is non-threatening in a way her previous collaboration meetings were not, not a casting couch or a sleazy producer in sight as Jessica smiles at her from her seat across the table. She introduces herself the same way—a warm smile and an exaggerated bend at the waist to showcase what many of her fans call an impressive rack.

She's sitting in the chair opposite Jessica, decidedly excited about what she came here to propose.

It's sex.

Marcus had the idea, admittedly—after a month and the four rolling payments a month's worth of OnlyFans existence has earned, he suggested she film a series of collaborations with some of the hottest, most popular creators in the space.

He'd borrowed the idea from porn, explaining that producers (like the still-oft-calling Frederick and Tomas) would build the brand of an emerging adult entertainer by pairing them in scenes with more established, experienced/famous stars.

Figuring a month (and the four rolling payments a month's worth of OnlyFans existence have earned) of content filmed/uploaded alone/featuring Rod Hardson have set the tone for the type of content her burgeoning fans can expect, he reasoned new content alongside a proven commodity like Jessica could only add value to her brand.

She proposes this to Jessica from across the café table as Jessica sips something that, between sips, she can't help but notice she looks good sipping.

Jessica is stunning in the way Influencers of her ilk sometimes-always are; she can't tell if she's attracted to her because Jessica is attractive or if she's attracted to her because of the business associating Jessica's established brand to her burgeoning brand will create. Either way, she prays the sex icon is interested; sex with someone other than Rod Hardson will surely attract what he's described in passing as one of the sex industry's greatest areas of interest—girl-on-equally-beautiful-girl.

She agrees, Jessica does, whispering an impressively sultry sounding

why not

before suggesting said arrangement take place at her studio/studio apartment next Friday night.

…

She's fucking excited, emerging from the passenger seat of Marcus's truck at Jessica's studio/studio apartment building on the Friday night that simply took too long to arrive.

The elevator ride to Jessica's studio/studio apartment takes forever, too; she spends the entirety of the ride analyzing herself in the mirror. Marcus sighs somewhere beside her, undoubtedly used to her fixation when faced with a reflective surface. She's dressed as well as she would have for a first date; the acknowledgment of the butterflies on dates too has her smiling ear to ear as she exits the elevator on the top floor.

Jessica's penthouse apartment is everything she'd hoped it would be. Eyes darting from perfectly appointed fixture to (equally) perfectly appointed fixture, she almost misses Jessica and her champagne-filled outstretched arms. She's late to the hug but vows to make up for it with an enthusiastically theatrical draining of the glass offered to her. Marcus exhibits a modicum of caution in the embracing of his—the hug more cordial and the taking of the champagne equally reserved.

Appreciating his decorum, she's nonetheless well into her second champagne flute by the time the tour has ended; she's marveling at the opulence OnlyFans can provide, and she's not lost on the fact that Marcus is offering one of his

told you so

Cheshire grins from behind the sanctity of his raised glass.

Jessica ends the tour in her celebrated/aforementioned studio, delivering a faux humility at the grandeur of her abode with the steely delivery of someone who has clearly done this before. She finds herself gasping audibly at the presentation of the studio—bathed in soft light, she's aware her reaction is secondary to tech-junkie Rod Hardson's enamored attention to the litany of sophisticated camera equipment.

She beckons an audience upon a decadent, clearly well-attended sofa, speaking in rehearsed tones of its origin from some store she's never heard of and of how it's covered in some leather she can't pronounce. She's sandwiched between Jessica and Marcus, and her champagne glass is filled for the third time in an hour, and her thoughts are racing faster than this sentence, and before she knows it...

CHAPTER SIXTEEN

In, but not over her head.

thoughts for Thots.

…there is a ball gag in her mouth.

Which, despite the obviousness of its presence in mouths more than hers, is totally okay.

It's okay because it's consensual, and it's okay because it was all part of Jessica's plan, and it's okay because this whole light BDSM thing is going to make her a ton of money.

An equally well-worn paddle intermittently explodes across the skin of her red little ass cheeks, and in between the hurts-so-bad-it-kinda-feels-good sensations she's remembering having seen content just like this proudly featured on Jessica's OnlyFans page. It's kind of her thing, the whole sexually aggressive/dominant thing, and—at Marcus's behest, she's the willing submissive for the willingly-submissive portion of tonight's champagne-fueled photoshoot/video recording.

So when she cries out, it's for the cameras, elaborating upon significant enough strikes, and, seeing a thumbs-up from Marcus across the room, clearly audible enough to be picked up on the recording.

The drool that escapes her mouth, despite Jessica's

you pathetic little pig

chastising in between

smack

smacks

of the paddle were predetermined to be an erotically appealing side-effect of having a rubber ball affixed in her mouth for the past twenty minutes.

The mock humiliation she's enduring, suggested after a fourth or fifth glass of champagne, is anything but; picturing the revenue that is bound to follow the uploading of tonight's bondage, she finds the experience oddly empowering—bent over and on all fours as she currently and most certainly is.

Jessica assured her—well before the placing of anal suppositories currently cycling in-and-out of what she's assured will be her own tight little revenue driver—that she retains full and total control of what content is to be distributed—a stark contrast to the control she lacks *right now*, what she can only picture as some horrible oversized dog-chew toy inserted forcefully into someplace she knows it was never intended to be.

She submits to rhythmic paddling and the senses-inflaming and entirely unrhythmic insertions, thinking back two champagne glasses to Jessica's proposal of future live-streaming opportunities. Figuring such decisions were better made sober, she acquiesced to tonight's recorded festivities, promising to table the discussion with Marcus first thing tomorrow morning.

Or, more accurately, afternoon, picturing the recovery needed for tonight's forthcoming hangover will require a distinct absence of morning participation.

She recalls Jessica making some comment of eventualities; remembers noting the confidence about her at various points in the evening, fully aware that she's done this exact thing before.

More than once.

Figuring it's simply one more thing to reflect on in an evening *full of*, she lets out another overly-enthusiastic cry as, somewhere behind her, Jessica does horribly experimental things to her body.

. . .

The shower Jessica offered—the shower she's enjoying right now—is being filmed by both Jessica and Marcus, because *why not*. Jessica claims that capturing content for future releases is of paramount importance; she's too drunk and too excited to realize that, ass reddened and makeup significantly smeared, she might have taken a little touch-up time in between.

Instead, she's focused only on lathering and imagining the ability to afford a shower just like this one, adored as she is and certainly will be by the multitudes of her fans happily parting with

$19.95

to see her shower in showers as fucking great as this one.

Just as she's reaching peak-fantasy, Jessica is suddenly in the shower and behind her and holding her as Marcus documents the encounter from a decidedly-not-showering (what with the camera equipment in his hand and all) position just outside.

He'd fit—which speaks to the splendor and the size of the shower she's no longer enjoying alone and speaks to the fact the champagne has her entertaining the idea of sharing her boyfriend with the woman she's sharing herself with (again)—and the whispers Jessica is whispering in her ear affirm he need not feel alone for long.

The water is warm, and so is her embrace, and long before the three of them climb into her necessarily large California King bed, she's grateful for both of her cuddle companions tonight.

. . .

Marcus is making mid-afternoon-hangover-appropriate breakfast, apparently having no trouble finding ingredients in Jessica's cavernous postmodern kitchen. She sits with their host, wrapped in what Jessica calls her favorite Versace robe, holding hands and reviewing the wealth of content created last night from her laptop.

In between photo two hundred nine and two hundred ten, she surprises her with a kiss, presented softly yet with no less passion than the kisses planted during last night's impromptu and unfortunately not-filmed bedtime threesome.

236

It gives her pause, this kiss, the first of its kind and not disguised as theatre for fans and subscribers who've yet to discover it. The warmth on her lips is sharp contrast to both the hate in her voice during last night's content creation and the fever in her attack in the sheets after; after enjoying this kiss and the ones that follow, she turns her attention to Marcus's recently presented Eggs Benedict and the suspicion that—when it comes to all things Jessica—she's taking every advantage of this startling opportunity.

CHAPTER SEVENTEEN

Turns out she's not the jealous type.

thoughts for Thots.

The video—edited to her approval (not that it required much in the way of touch-ups or post-production) goes out to her OnlyFans sometime the following Monday. Jessica shares it over her socials also—to say it does well is an understatement.

Between the submission clip, shower video, and dozens of photos captured throughout last Friday's particularly carnal evening, she's awash with content to upload at her discretion.

Discretion, which, she's learning, she may not have all that much of.

In the time since emerging/almost crawling from Jessica's studio/studio apartment, Marcus has approached conversation—particularly conversation related to the events of the evening—with the reservation of a man with a guilty conscience. Which, given his chosen profession, and paired with his proven lack of disdain for her sleeping with other performers in the porn space, seems odd and inconsistent with his recent behavior.

She allows him to tiptoe around what is proving to be a financially fortuitous elephant-in-the-room *until* he retreats to the sanctity of the couch and his video game controller. Sensing a lack of communication/quality time/any human interaction at all on the horizon, she finds a familiar position beside him on the sofa, curling up into the ball that had her first hear of OnlyFans, and prays this revelation has the same outcome.

He explains some forty minutes (and, she notes, keeping a watchful eye on the open laptop on the coffee table, 10 OnlyFans subscribers) later, expressing his fears that she will harbor some latent resentment for his involvement in Friday's threesome.

More than once

More than twice, even

his relationships with women—even women equally employed in the adult entertainment industry—have been affected over time by his occasional employment requirement of fucking other women.

Upon the revelation, he places the video game controller down, as if emphasizing, for some dramatic effect, the consequences of his continued engagement in both relationships and porn. He's surprised, apparently, at her reaction—the sum total of his vocalized fears met with a chuckle and a playful kick, uncoiling as she is from her side of the couch.

She embraces him moments later, still laughing and now at his resulting near-fall from the sofa, her kick apparently delivered with an enthusiasm he was not prepared for.

She assures him, between breaths better served catching hers and for the intermittent fits of laughter, that she's far from jealous, recounting his penetration of Jessica amongst drunken memories of *her* penetration of Jessica (thanks to the toys she was allowed to borrow and the role reversal she was allowed to enact.) Maybe her excitement at the monetization of experience a young woman in a new, big city should be allowed to discover is clouding formerly-formed opinions; perhaps the small-town girl who got on a bus had *all of this* inside her all along. Either way, she's in love and probably with him, and certainly with this industry she's fallen into, any memories of the abject horror she first regarded pornography with replaced with dollar signs in her mind and--as subscribers continue to join from the laptop on the coffee table across from the sofa they're now making out on--her bank account too.

He swears she's nothing like the other ones, the ones that led him to want her out of the traditional porn industry in a way he never had before, even in the past relationships with porn stars, porn stars who foolishly felt some kind of way when he was fucking other porn stars.

So while she sincerely appreciated his feelings and the conversation that led her away from the path she'd been traveling down, she's maybe more appreciative of the level of care he continues to show her, his worries of fucking other women—part of his job or not—and the cumulative effect on her psyche energy entirely wasted. Energy, she reminds him right there on his usually-reserved-for-video-games-and-significant-talks-couch—that would be better utilized *elsewhere*.

CHAPTER EIGHTEEN

A distinct lack of (probably unnecessary anyways) upgrades.

thoughts for Thots.

Jessica has fake hair. (Glue-ins.)

Jessica has fake eyelashes. (Mink.)

Jessica has fake cheekbones. (Collagen injections.)

Jessica has a new nose. (Plastic surgery #1.)

Jessica has fake tits. (Plastic surgeries #2 and #3.)

Jessica has had her floating ribs removed. (!)

Jessica has a fake fat ass. (Fat injections, which she tells her is the best/safest way.)

Legal way, anyways—turns out she's learned of a doctor who will inject usually-reserved-for-fake-tits-silicone into a paying customer's ass at an appropriately seedy motel room not far from his clinic—but she's yet to see any of the *results*, so she's hesitant to recommend going this route.

Listening to Jessica detail the various procedures she's undergone to become the desirable Influencer/mogul she has become, she's looking in the mirror and, quite frankly, can't think of an 'upgrade' procedure worth subjecting herself to.

In the week since her first submission video went live on OnlyFans, the traffic to her subscription-based site has skyrocketed. She's counting the hours until that first week's earnings are deposited directly into her bank account—earnings that will no doubt amount to the largest earnings of her young life. Enough to pay for the litany of upgrades Jessica softly suggests she look into, upgrades she's entirely sure she has zero interest in.

The mirror—and thousands of fans on Instagram and scores of fans on OnlyFans and maybe most importantly Marcus—assure her that her raven black hair doesn't need tinting and that her almond-shaped eyes have eyelashes that are long enough and that her perfectly shaped somehow-still-perky-C-cup breasts only *add* to her youthful appearance, no Frankenstein-style bolt-ons needed. Her nose, 'The Duchess' in shape (according to the Plastic Surgeon who set it following a particularly nasty gymnastics fail when she was eleven) is among the most desirable and requested by unfortunately-appointed clients who frequent his clinic, so no need there. Her cheekbones are sufficiently high, her jawline handsomely set—her ass, she has been told on multiple occasions, is just the right kind/amount of *fat*.

In the days since reassuring Marcus that, post impromptu orgy, she feels no type of way regarding his interactions with what could amount to her new best friend, Jessica has been a near-constant presence in their lives. Today, she's at their place and somewhere just outside the bathroom and the bathroom mirror she's examining herself in, having assured her that her Plastic Surgeon is the best Plastic Surgeon and that she could schedule a consultation post-haste.

She politely declined Jessica's invitation before retreating to the sanctity of the bathroom, mirror reaffirming her gut feeling that

no

she won't be altering any aspect of her physical appearance in order to push an already-lucrative revenue stream and

no

she won't be needing any tattoos, either, despite Jessica's claim that girls with plentiful ink earn more.

She exits the bathroom only after Jessica's disclosure that she'll be paying for the lunch she's taking her and Marcus to, steadfast and resolute in regards to the fact that her body is just fucking fine the way it is.

CHAPTER NINETEEN

Secure the fucking bag.

thoughts for Thots.

If imitation is the sincerest form of flattery, *this*—downright impersonation—should have her feeling significantly flattered. Jessica tells her it's a good thing, these multiple fake accounts showing up almost daily on Instagram—that despite their collective existence and links to fake paid accounts (or, at the very least, real paid accounts that don't pay her), it's a near-necessary evil in pursuit of something called 'Account Verification.'

According to Jessica, the 'little blue check' that shows up beside someone's Instagram account name is the rite of passage every worthwhile Influencer or entertainer or musician or adult industry worker should strive to achieve—and that, by virtue of these multiple fake accounts pretending to be her, her time is clearly now.

She doesn't really see the point, her social media audience growing daily and her paid account paying nicely, but Jessica is the expert, and so she allows her to navigate to the

Request Verification

button hidden away somewhere in her account settings, and—with the pressing of said button—waits to be told whether or not her thousands and thousands-strong audience merits admittance into what she can only equate to the cool-kids-in-school club.

It's trite, and it's ridiculous, and, to be frank, she feels it is somewhat beneath her, but Jessica has a blue check, and Marcus says he applies for his near-monthly, and so she reluctantly joins the plethora of Instagram accounts begging for acceptance.

While she waits, Jessica suggests shopping; a celebration of recent successes meriting spending some of her newly acquired money. She agrees, but only after a phone call to Marcus, a phone call, and a request to set up an appointment with a Financial Planner.

She grew up poor—dirt poor—in some small town back somewhere, the kind of place where investments amounted to four-letter words. She reasons that is part of the reason she got on that bus in the first place, leaving

maybe Dakota

maybe Vancouver

maybe West Virginia, New Hampshire

maybe Toronto, maybe Dallas

the small town near the now-inconsequential city she swears she'll never go back to, living amongst the now-inconsequential people she swore she would never end up like.

So she agrees to shop with Jessica, but only after ensuring the bulk of her newly-acquired capital is safely and responsibly secured, future—having watched the not-fortunes of the kids she grew up with—stabilized the way she always prayed it would be.

...

The shoes are pretty, shopping with Jessica in the kinds of stores she'd only imagined herself shopping in—between rows of hard-to-pronounce Italian designer labels, she's wondering what types of real estate she's going to invest in, the heels she buys she envisions wearing on trips to see investment properties.

CHAPTER TWENTY

Cam girl, too.

thoughts for Thots.

It's a logical progression, Jessica says.

A different level of connectivity and connectivity is the key to maximizing revenue generation with her (now) legion of adoring fans.

Jessica says something about brand diversification, and it sounds good, and it makes sense, so she listens to Jessica in the way she realizes that Jessica is worth listening to.

Sometimes.

She suggests the requisite major players in the cam space—Chaturbate.com, Pornhub's PornLive.com, myfreecams.com (on which Jessica herself is one of the larger accounts) reviewing each with Marcus and appreciating his insight, himself a formerly-more-frequent-but-still-sometimes-present feature on the aforementioned PornLive.com. Jessica, having claimed to earn up to forty-thousand per month at her peak, leans heavily on the idea that she broadcast near-daily; settling on PornLive.com (due in part to crossover opportunities with Rod Hardson and due in part to the fact that both her produced porn videos live on the site) she sets up her account, eager to see how much 'Gold' (--the online currency converted to cash payment used on the platform) her newfound channel can mine.

Marcus helps facilitate the conversation with the appropriate administrators the way he helps facilitate many of her important-figure-for-her-future considerations, and—within a week—she's set up at their home and about to broadcast for the very first time.

She's nervous—the better part of the past week spent direct messaging her most loyal followers and offering them access to a 'soft launch'—fully aware that their investment on the OnlyFans platform does not guarantee financial support on this new venture. Jessica assures her that, even though they can already see the entirety of her on the previous paid platform—not to mention the proper Pornhub site—the interactivity with live streaming will allow for connectivity in a way other mediums cannot.

Thoughts of putting herself out there, literally and live, and *not* having Gold tokens virtually thrown her way are small—small but present in the back of her mind. Having borrowed one of Jessica's favorite vibrators, she thumbs the *on* button and motions with a nod of her head that Marcus does the same, commencing her PornLive.com debut and hoping fans of *I've Been A Bad Girl 4* and *Pornstars Gone Wild* are online and in the mood for some keyboard-driven conversation.

…

She starts slow.

From across the room, Marcus indicates she's live and that the first of her fans are tuning in, striding towards her and positioning the laptop in a way that will allow her to read their comments, one hand dedicated to her remote keyboard while one hand attends Jessica's favorite vibrator.

She fakes her best sex face, eyes scanning the screen to count her audience members and pleasantly discovering that

43 people

instantly tuned into this, her first live performance.

Jessica had told her that many of her Instagram and OnlyFans supporters would be amongst the first to view—that visitors happening by the host site would be given a menu of performing-live rooms, but that established performers would be given priority designation towards the top of the screen. The key, she said, to attract new fans with no prior knowledge was the screenshot on her room profile—and that the more scandalous the pic, the more attractive the profile.

Given the

68 people

now watching her stumble through her introduction, she figures she chose well.

Traditionally, she's told, the idea is to start slow—clothed, but provocatively—and offer a menu of interactive performance 'milestones' for her viewers to reach given their cumulative Gold. One of the advantages of PornLive.com over other platforms—Jessica's myfreecams.com included—is the lack of text debris on the screen, leaving her free and unencumbered to guide the performance as she pleases.

So she begins naked and masturbating, her campaign designed to shock and awe,

89 people

appreciating her direct approach, Gold virtually raining down on her by minute five, minute ten featuring an appearance from Rod Hardson, minute-thirty four and

156 people

witness to a baby oil infused climax.

…

The stream ends, having reached a peak (minute twenty-four) total of nearly two hundred fans. She shudders, effects of orgasm number two, and the cold Marcus's insistence on year-round air conditioning have upon baby oil soaked skin; his post-live-stream embrace does wonders to warm her.

Thoughts of debasing herself for the gratification of the unwashed masses turns her on; thoughts of unwashed masses tipping handsomely turns her on even more. Marcus tells her that, based on one Gold being equal to one US dollar, she just earned a sizeable down payment towards her next series of investments…and that, for her next show, adding a Pay-Per-Minute chat room could *double* her near-hour performance earnings.

She tells him she'll entertain the idea, politely excusing

herself for the sanctity of a much-needed shower. Locking the bathroom door, she takes the duration of the water warming in the shower to note two very important details:

she's still shaking, equal parts excitement and air conditioning

and

the amount of new followers and new Direct Messages on her social feeds that are commenting on her performance tells her that she'll never be able to keep her platforms separate again.

CHAPTER TWENTY ONE

Super logical
next steps.

thoughts for Thots.

More is more

is what Jessica is always saying

and

more

might equate, to her, to more uploaded content—and while content is certainly her primary revenue driver, more is good advice in terms of investments and responsible allocation of revenue earned.

So she sits *here*, the office of one James A Mueller, a prominent 'Financial Strategist' at Birchtree Capital Group, LLC, waiting on a week's-planned meeting and to discuss what to do with the jaw-dropping amount of money she's accrued over the past few months.

Marcus shifts uncomfortably beside her, his impressive six foot four frame grossly overqualified to fit the restrictions of the imported leather chair he semi-impatiently waits in. Birchtree—like so many of his recommendations as of late—appears to be a good one, widely regarded as the largest and most well-known private equity firm in the city. Primarily focused on the entertainment industry, the firm's assets—at least, according to the website she reads on her phone from the comfort of her appropriately-sized imported leather waiting chair—exceed $110 billion.

Private equity (he had explained over a forty-minute conversation that really only needed the first five to convince her) was advantageous due to higher returns than the public market typically provides. He'd mentioned something about private equity funds having a higher degree of risk due to the inherent volatility of the…*something*; she recalls making her mind up directly after hearing the higher reward portion of the conversation, insisted he pick up the phone and arrange the meeting that led them here.

Here where they wait, and with a noticeably growing disdain often associated with the nu-wealthy type that feel above waiting. She's reaching peak frustration when the door to the waiting room opens, subtly reminding her of how she felt waiting on that casting couch all those months ago, the presence of Frederick and Tomas at once dispelling and compounding her anxiety. This time, the figure emerging from behind the door is neither sleazy porn producer or male—rather an attractive, would-do-well-in-porn female who beckons they follow with a smile better suited for film. As she and Marcus navigate the corridors of Birchtree Capital, LLC, behind the appropriately pleasant secretary, she finds herself staring at her ass and noting the effects her duration in the adult entertainment industry seems to be having on her worldview.

The thought proves fleeting. As they reach their destination at the end of the post-modern, ecru painted hallway, they're guided into a post-modern, ecru painted office. An office curiously decorated with vintage furniture and bohemian appointments, reds, and purples on the floors a stark contrast to the sparse, shades-of-grey trappings of the waiting rooms and hallways. The pleasant-faced secretary guides them over an impressively-sized floor rug and across a series of thoughtfully strewn animal hides to the leather-backed chairs opposite a rich mahogany desk and what could only be one James A Mueller.

He's the color of the rug, a rich red, rising from behind the rich red of his mahogany desk to greet them, an enthusiastic grin spread across his private-equity-firm-handsome features.

His

pleasure to meet you

is followed with a

wait—I recognize that face

and the appropriate scanning of her face and everything beneath it, indicating

    a)   it's not just her face he recognizes

and

    b)   he's the type of investor someone in her position can certainly work with.

The pleasantries continue unabated, the secretary retreating after promising to return with hallway-ordered mineral water. James A Mueller eagerly shakes Marcus's hand after warmly embracing her and commending her performance in *I've Been A Bad Girl 4*. He's decidedly not what she'd envisioned, picturing the majority of financial industry workers to be the out-of-touch senior citizens she'd dealt with in her limited dealings with bankers back home. The fact he's familiar—and comfortable—with her line of work emboldens her as they sit to commence conversation; despite Marcus's assurances that firms like Birchtree deal with entertainment industry types, she'd assumed entertainment industry types did not include her type of entertainment.

Across his mahogany desk, framed by the taxidermized wildlife bookending the laptop and mineral water strewn surface, James A Mueller is beaming, introducing her to concepts like

two and twenty

(--something about the percentage of assets under management and the annual fee the firm will charge, and the twenty percent standard performance fee above benchmark)

and

waterfall distribution.

He's detailing the latter, and about how he'll allocate capital gains of the investment pool he'll have her join, but she's focused more on the curiosities of his byzantine office and the richness of his tan, already having decided that James A Mueller is *her* investor and that it's more to do with his complicated investment terms than his dimples.

He asks

how much

and it's how much would she like to begin investing with, and it's how much does she trust him, and by extension, Birchtree Capital Group, LLC, and she turns to a smiling Marcus, Jessica, and her

more is more

truisms are ringing through her head.

After a brief conversation and a brief sip of refreshing mineral water, it's

a lot

and the commencement of the procedures that—by the time they leave James A Mueller and his richly-appointed office—have her confident in the foundations of what will surely become her empire.

CHAPTER TWENTY TWO

No. No...and... goodbye

thoughts for Thots.

She's not having sex for money.

Jessica tried to talk her into it the way Jessica always tries to talk her into it, assurances of sexually transmitted disease screens and non-disclosure agreements, and insisting that many of the OnlyFans tipping whales were aware of the standard operating procedures for proceedings like this.

She reasons James A Mueller would pay, having heard of her partnership with Birchtree Capital Group, LLC and equating everything back to sex the way she always does—she politely insists on keeping business separate from her businesses associated with pleasure, politely insisting the way she has to when Jessica gets going like *this*.

She flutters her fucking seafoam green eyes the way she does when the fight is all but lost, some primordial last-ditch effort to win the battle with her substantial beauty. Having recognized the pattern, she redirects her with inquiries about shopping excursions, putting to proverbial bed any further conversation regarding bedding her fans for money. Money she's acquiring at a dizzying pace, the need for extracurricular prostitution-related activities almost non-existent. Which reminds her to call the still-calling Frederick and Tomas back, call them back and thank them for the roles they played in her ascension here, budding independent mogul, sipping champagne on the balcony of the home she shares with Marcus, first of many homes she's certain she's bound to own.

CHAPTER TWENTY THREE

Too much

Not enough.

thoughts for Thots.

They tell her they're happy for her

and

she tells them she misses them

and

as far as she can tell, neither of them are lying.

Frederick and Tomas sit across the living room coffee table from her, invited over, and to talk the way she assumes friends do. They're not—friends—and maybe it's the isolation, months spent shooting content with only Marcus (and occasionally his alter-ego) and Jessica and sometimes James A Mueller to keep her company, but their relatively fresh presence in her living room has her feeling all kinds of warm and fuzzy.

They look good—relatively speaking—or at least as good as two (post?) middle-aged, balding, feverishly-perspiring-even-in-air-conditioning porn producers can look, bathed in soft living room lighting and offered cordial coffee by a doting, domestically amazing Marcus.

So yes, Tomas and his unusually long forehead are showcasing the type of perspiration that she's come to associate with a want to ask something of her; his sausage-like fingers seem to shake as they reach for Marcus and his offered mug—this does little to erode the must-be-genuine feeling of happiness she's feeling and to be seated here with the pair of them.

She cuts the palpable tension with a

'Midwestern plain' did okay, huh

joke and reference to one of the label they'd associated with her, their collective calling her

Goddess

and reminding her of how they knew she'd be a star dissipating any lingering feelings of unease. They converse in excited, hurried tones over plentiful caffeinated top-ups; telling her of how they've had to settle for former

I've Been A Bad Girl

series lead Roxanne Von Slut in the wake of their post-departure productions and of how the lawsuit against Hollywood Rick is progressing before getting down to the business they came here for—the business that bore month's worth of unanswered calls and copious, exacerbated voicemails.

We want you back

in tone and literally, spoken by both and around continued praising of her OnlyFans and cam girl successes. She smiles, feigning a need to hear more in the way of compliments, and they elaborate extensively—Tomas detailing his vision of a new series of contracted, big-budget productions, based entirely around her ascent to what he pleasingly calls her *dominance of the porn-pop-culture zeitgeist.*

Frederick chimes in with an outline that spans at least four filmed scenes—each building upon and informing the other

like the Marvel movies

a now overly-caffeinated Tomas adds, the intent to bring the fanbase she's acquired along as the scripted storyline evolves. It sounds intriguing—particularly when they get to the compensation part of the proposal, her mind already racing and at the investment opportunities that would open up to her with the added, guaranteed revenue.

They reach the end of their half-scripted presentation, Frederick even referring to storyboards he's grabbed from the decidedly feminine looking satchel he's rested beside him on the couch. Ascertaining her interest based on what she's purposefully keeping as a reserved veneer, they exchange glances and nods before Tomas opens his mouth,

and

drawn-out suspensefully and indicating they've saved the sweetest part of the pitch for last.

We've made a few calls.

She politely encourages them to continue

We can get you the hosting gig at the AVN's next year.

This, she admits—and despite her attempts at maintaining a poker face, with a nearly audible gasp—she did not see coming.

The 'Oscars of Porn,' the Adult Video News awards, sponsored by industry trade bible AVN, represent the absolute pinnacle in American pornographic achievement. Mainstream entertainers, comedians, or singers typically occupy the hosting duties; only the upper echelon of porn-related personalities are ever offered the hosting or co-hosting gig.

Marcus—doing far less to contain his excitement—hugs a taken-by-surprise (and still no doubt traumatized by the Hollywood Rick assault) Tomas while Frederick grins the kind of

I know, right

grin that indicates he really *does* know.

She offers a not really restrained

Yes

because how could she not; agreeing and in principle to star in a blockbuster series of high quality, big-budget pornographic films—her own

cinematic universe

Frederick shouts as they embrace, the four of them spilling coffee and sharing hugs and marveling at how the girl that got on that bus less than a year ago grew up to host the motherfucking AVN's.

…

She separates only after running out of breath, collecting herself and still holding onto an exhausted Frederick, arms outstretched and scanning the eyes of the three of them, before parting perfectly pouty lips to mouth a subtle

Just one more thing….

CHAPTER TWENTY FOUR

Bo$$ Bitch.

thoughts for Thots.

The chair she sits in has writing on the back, and the writing says

Producer.

The writing says

Producer

in big, bold, capital white letters—producer because she *is* and producer because it was the sole condition that needed to be met before she fully committed to *this*

Day One

of shooting the first of what will become four films in a shared universe of Hollywood quality (--or at least foreign cinema quality) productions centered solely on her.

Reclining in her appropriately-labeled-but-missing-the-word

Star

chair, she takes a moment to appreciate her path back here and how—after telling herself she was done with traditional porn—all it took was building a tiny little independent empire to come back and conquer it.

Her schedule may be a touch full over the next few months, twice-weekly OnlyFans uploads and at least as many cam shows bookending her days (and nights) either filming for the movie or going over the day's content in *post*—but busy is good, and she appreciates the opportunity to take on a greater understanding of the machinations involved behind the scenes while honoring her commitments in front of the camera.

She figures the knowledge she gains will only further her independent business ventures, the eventual release of her series only raising her profile and—hopefully—her already plentiful amount of monthly paid subscribers.

She moves—literally between the producer's chair she produces from to the bed the afternoon's scene is to be filmed on; metaphorically between spaces someone with her relative *newness* shouldn't be able to, hosting and producing and calling the shots with a confidence that belies what Jessica reminds her are relatively short years.

Marcus tells her he's proud of her, and he tells her that he's never seen anything like it and—right now—Rod Hardson tells her to

bite that fucking pillow

because he's her co-star in the scene they're shooting

Day One

of ensuring she's the kind of famous even people back home have heard of.

Somewhere over her left shoulder—and she can't see exactly where, what with her face buried in the pillow Rod Hardson instructed she bury it in—Jessica is lecturing some poor production assistant that the set design is all wrong. She's relatively sure that it won't be picked up by the boom mike she's being aggressively fucked under, but it's audible to her and over the names Rod Hardson is calling her, names they agreed upon (and not without a healthy amount of laughter) in last night's meeting with the director.

She reminds herself to remind Jessica that she's here to observe and *only*, efforts to inject her into the films meeting a degree of resistance from Tomas and Frederick and the director, who—judging by the abrupt

Cut

that abruptly ruins any attempt to relax and enjoy the pounding that Rod Hardson was in the middle of—has also overheard her unwarranted interjections.

She sighs, removing herself from Rod and the bed and pretending she's not thrilled to be involved in the kind of production where a director can call *cut*, robing herself as a now-shaking production assistant offers her a robe and reminding herself that—just because this experience is amazing—doesn't mean that it will be easy.

. . .

She finds Jessica near where the craft services table would be if Tomas hadn't been terrified into never ordering craft services ever again. She gets to her before the director, mercifully, grabbing her by the arm and escorting her

--something, she notes with a smirk, she would always dream of being able to do—and weathering her wine-infused explanations until they're well out of range of the director and his justified impatience.

When confronted about her...influence...on set, Jessica bats those fucking seafoam green eyes and justifies her 'delicate' interjections as the warranted and requested observations of a seasoned professional.

Realizing that her ability to get through to her will be next to impossible, she changes tactics, reassuring Jessica that she's having positive feedback in regards to her proposed character's introduction to what will be Episode 2, promising her with a batting of her equally-appeasing eyes that she'll appear on Jessica's live cam show tonight.

This does wonders to distract her—she encourages her to hurry home and prepare the dungeon, realizing the light S&M beating she's sure to endure later is worth it, Jessica's need to control better served in the privacy of her penthouse studio/studio apartment than *here*, the set she's sure the director is already looking for her on.

She's back on the bed, face-down biting the pillow minutes later, satisfied and satisfying Rod Hardson and appreciating (between the poundings) her newfound producer's ability to handle small, circumstantial crises.

Turns out this is just one more thing she's good at, fitting bookend to her first discovered talents; the ability to visualize a better life and the bravery to buy a bus ticket.

CHAPTER TWENTY FIVE

Money Moves.

thoughts for Thots.

She doesn't need money.

That doesn't mean she doesn't *want* money, and so she's *here*, an apartment on the West Side/Best Side, investing in real estate the way, she figures, motherfucking media moguls do.

It's expensive and *too*, but the view is phenomenal, and the surrounding properties have increased in value dramatically over the past five years, and in five years, it will be worth exponentially more, and so she invests, adding this to a healthy portfolio that ensures her retirement from the adult film industry can be whenever she wants it to be.

The semi-surprised-but-no-less-elated real estate agent interjects, wondering aloud if she would like to discuss particulars before placing an offer, reminding her in hushed tones that bully offers these days could see the property go for tens of thousands over asking.

She turns to face him, already aware that beside her, Marcus is smirking his this-fool-shouldn't-have-challenged-her smirk, analyzing his diminutive features, weak jawline, and slightly-too-close-together eyes that he—despite showcasing properties here on the West Side/Best Side—lacks the decorum necessary to dealing with boss bitches like her.

She smiles, the kind of smile she's used to smiling when she wants to weaken men like him, speaking softly and yet still directly that she'll

beat the top offer by five percent

and that she would prefer to have this property acquired by Friday.

He stutters over his somewhat inconsequential response; she catches his promise to get the deal done as she enters the elevator, her brand new Mercedes Benz G-Class waiting for her downstairs. Sophisticated elegance powers her all the way home, first of many she's sure she will sell, her and Marcus moving and up in a world she can suddenly feel she was born to belong to.

CHAPTER TWENTY SIX

Jessica.

thoughts for Thots.

Jessica is kind of a lot.

The cause of ever-increasing consternation, she's—after much delicate finessing on her part—inserted herself into Episode Two, arriving for her first official day with a subtlety reminiscent of a rabid raccoon in a dumpster fire.

Twenty-six minutes late for her call time, she's already well on her way to infuriating the director and Tomas and Frederick and, well, *her*—or at least the her that is producing *this*, the scene that now means all remaining scenes will shoot late.

Jessica is fighting with the director regarding the 'harsh' lighting, and Jessica is fighting with Tomas and the costume designer regarding perceived imperfections with her costume, and, momentarily, Jessica will be fighting with her unless she gets on all fours the way the scene says she's supposed to.

Beside her, Marcus sighs his seventy-sixth sigh of the past twenty-seven (and counting) minutes, his ability to 'perform' for the duration of the required scene meaning he'll likely need another tiny blue pill. She's not crazy about his consumption of Viagra, concerned about the potential long-term ramifications—he calls it one of his occupational hazards and tells her to be thankful and flattered he never needs the assist when performing with/for her.

So Marcus is losing his famous Rod Hardson hardon, and Tomas is losing whatever precious little remains of his hair, and the director is rapidly losing his desire to keep this bitch in his movie and, once again, it falls on *her* to produce a dramatically different attitude than the one Jessica seems intent on showcasing.

She almost gets it, Jessica's rampant and all-consuming need for control the unfortunate by-product of a woman who has built an empire based solely on will. And on an independent—hell, defiant—attitude. And on all the alcohol in the city.

So when she finds herself grabbing the embattled starlet by the arm, it is with a reservation borne of understanding and care. Care, because she might very well be the only friend in the world and care because she is hyper-aware that she's a tiny little Adderall addiction away from turning out just like *this*.

Jessica assures her that everything is all right the way Jessica assures her everything is all right every time they're forced to take a walk; she's memorized the steps they'll take before the mock light-headedness is blamed for her outburst. Recognizing what is at stake (--namely her latest retirement fund and whatever preceding career in film production she's earned), she begins the *give your fucking head a shake*

conversation with decidedly less incendiary words, not entirely confident that she won't end up here. Having learned a valuable lesson from the last time, she knows there will be no conciliatory submission live cam later; if Jessica wants to remain a part of Episode Two, she's going to need to relinquish a modicum of the control she so desperately clings to.

She starts slow, measured tones and a batting of her equally impressive eyes and affirmations that

yes

you're going to kill it

and

you look so fucking hot in that

and

they're going to dim the light in post-production.

(She remains relatively astonished at her objections to the lighting; this is a woman who live-cams daily in 4K broadcasted streams, any imperfections real or perceived are certainly nothing new to her audience.)

She nods in mock understanding when Jessica claims the director is working

to sabotage my ascendant emergence into porn proper

and

that little assistant bitch has been telling Tomas I'm drunk

and

can you believe that

and

I'm not drunk

and

just a little nervous

and

the batting of those fucking seafoam green eyes that she's so used to convincing people with. She takes her rebuttals in stride, having heard them before and on multiple occasions, her visitations on the set of Episode One already well-documented and presented in the production meetings/wars she had to attend/win in order to end up *here*.

She's pleased and maybe even a little surprised in her ability to keep composure, recognizing the half-hour lost is quickly looking to grow exponentially.

Minute thirty-two and her sigh is forced and, she's sure, reminiscent of the hundreds Marcus has sighed by now, erection fading like her ability to keep Jessica in this fucking movie.

Running out of options, she weighs her friendship with Jessica against the opportunities she's on the verge of losing...

And she slaps that bitch in the face.

Hard, and just enough to stop her in her tracks, whatever

everyone's fault but mine

excuse falling faster than the line of spittle that escapes her perfectly-plumped lips. Drawing her hand back, she takes note of how it stings, the filler in Jessica's perfectly-filled cheeks doubtless offering resistance to the force of her strike.

She shrieks, Jessica does, and it's one of those overly theatrical shrieks better suited for the movie set they're now officially really fucking late to.

She explains this to the frozen-in-shock face she's facing

because of you, the whole day's shoot is fucked

and

you're not going to ruin this for me

and

one more fucking stunt, and you're off the movie

as authoritatively as she can when invested in saving the friendship she just slapped in the proverbial face.

The face she just literally slapped is still frozen in place, shriek having faded to a look of…something she really can't tell, Jessica frozen and staring at her with fucking seafoam green eyes and one rosy cheek.

A minute passes, a minute filled with micro-reminders to remain resolute, steadfast as she is in her desire to go back and resume filming the way she desperately needs to.

She's intent on giving Jessica the benefit of another seventeen seconds before returning to what she can only imagine is a furious director and a limp-dicked Rod Hardson when, without a word of contention, Jessica grabs her natural, filler-less cheeks and kisses her on the lips.

Hard, like the slap, and with a passion, she imagines one usually associates with pleasure and not the pain she's just physically caused her.

So Jessica kisses her, minute thirty-four from her call time thirty-four contested minutes ago, and she doesn't stop until minute thirty-five, when she abruptly withdraws, looking at her with tear-filled fucking seafoam green eyes, and says *okay*

before wordlessly marching back to the set, completing
the day's scene, and the rest of the scenes that follow
without so much as a hint of resistance.

CHAPTER TWENTY SEVEN

Ball gowns and Back home baggage.

thoughts for Thots.

Turns out that running an empire is exhausting.

Principal filming has finished; her acting commitments are—for the moment and barring any unforeseen reshoots—over and done.

Producing, she's learning, is in many ways *harder*, working closely with Frederick and Tomas and the editing team, and ensuring what was captured on high definition video translates to a high quality, finished product.

Which means her days are full, nights still occupied with live shows and content creation for her surging OnlyFans—early rehearsals and prep for the upcoming AVN awards occupying the free time previously allocated to Marcus and some semblance of a personal life. There's meetings with James A Mueller to discuss money and hedge funds and the distribution of said money; Jessica (who has been, miraculously, well-behaved for the past few months) has been demanding time for awards show dress shopping and the ghosts previously known as family have been coming out of the proverbial woodwork and requesting, to her, unnecessary reconciliations.

She's reasonably sure that these requests coincide nicely with the erosion of her anonymity, and so they're relegated to the very bottom of what is becoming a daunting to-do list.

Today is Tuesday, and unmercifully; unmerciful Tuesday is looking to be as jam-packed as Monday, the first in forever that the comments on her latest Instagram post were more

you look tired

than

you look hot.

She's too busy to heed any of Marcus's well-intentioned requests for a bit of reprieve—it isn't until Jessica calls for the sixth time that she listens to someone other than herself, clearing a calendar full of terribly-important appointments and agreeing to a little lunch and a little more shopping.

...

Jessica is in control.

And, by extension, heaven—commanding she tries on what has to be the twelfth in a series of increasingly revealing and increasingly expensive dresses.

It reminds her of high school prom back home, back home forefront of her troubled mind, and maybe because back home has been calling lately and for the first time since she bought a ticket for that bus.

So her thoughts are heavy, and her dresses are increasingly anything but, standing half-naked and a little cold here on the floor at Givenchy and decidedly more uncomfortable than the half (or more) naked she is on the internet and daily and comfortably.

She's admittedly a little tired and maybe a little overworked, and somewhere underneath her, Jessica is working too, pulling at what she calls the

entirely too much fabric, this won't do

fringe at the bottom of her thirteenth-*maybe* AVN awards opening-segment-proposed outfit.

She needs a break, and not just from the array of ribcage-tightening-sheer-fabric-patterned materials smothering her money-making curves; she tells Jessica

this is the one

more out of defeat than the desire to wear this dress over the near-countless others she's been presented, excusing herself to the relative sanctity of the dressing room. She slides the curtain separating her from Jessica and the show floor with authority, collapsing on the Givenchy day-bed that of-course-the-dressing-room-has, ignoring the fact that the dressing room is the size of her parent's house back home and ignoring the fact that she's thinking of her parent's house back home.

Finally admitting exhaustion, she fights the urge to sleep, thumbing through a healthy amount of missed calls and, finding Marcus's name among the litany of *Jessicas* and *Back Homes* and the moment he picks up, ring three and dependable as *always* the first thing she says after

Hello

and

baby

and

his

hello baby

back,

is

baby, I need a break,

his

I know, baby—I've got a plan

just the reassurance she needs, closing the call and her eyes and allowing sleep to take her and her time the way seemingly everyone in the whole wide world *wants* to.

CHAPTER TWENTY EIGHT

(Spoiler.)

thoughts for Thots.

Marcus is on one knee, and his hand is in his pocket, and he's holding her hand with his free one and, suddenly, her heart is racing maybe the fastest it has ever raced because the hand in the pocket is making its way out again and—when it does—

there's a pretty big fucking box in it.

And she's always thought her name was plain and insignificant and boring, but the way he's saying it

Sarah

and *right now,* it's maybe the sweetest it has ever sounded.

For the first time in her life, she's okay with her name— her real name, and not the porn/stage name she's become accustomed to hearing over the past year

Sarah

sounding better than

Tahlia

for the first time because the man saying it is the man she loves, the man she loves and has built an empire with, an anchor that came into her life at a time when she so desperately needed one.

(She's entirely confident that she'd have been equally successful on her own, thank you very much, but her ascension to the top of the adult entertainment space has been significantly more fun, having someone to share it with.)

And right now, the man she shares her life with is opening the pretty big fucking box with both hands, the hand that held his moving to cover her mouth and the sound that escapes it

because he opens the box, all

will you marry me

as he reveals the biggest fucking diamond she's ever seen.

She's relatively sure that she says

yes

instantly and with resounding confidence; to be honest, she can't hear, and she can't tell, and she may very well be on the verge of fainting, incapable of feeling much but the tears of joy streaming down her perfectly plumped, non-filler filled cheeks.

Marcus places the ring on her finger and rises to meet/catch her, tears maybe streaming down his face too—she can't tell because her vision is blurry and his face is smothering hers, the kisses that come coming fast and with a passion befitting the moment.

The moments that pass next take half-forever; she's sure that, later in life, she will appreciate the many moments the moments take, in his arms and happy, perfect ending to a year full of increasingly memorable milestones.

...

She's sitting across a fancy restaurant table from her family.

Well, the people responsible for creating her—her family sits beside her, Jessica still gushing about the size of the ring, and Marcus doing his best to downplay the only-embarrassing-in-certain-company specifics regarding his employment.

Across the table, the people responsible for creating Sarah look appropriately astonished, admitting that they had not followed the specifics of her employment post-small-town somewhere. She's thankful she gave it to them in broad-strokes and doses, omitting the hardcore porn part of film-series-star and lightly touching on the reputation of the OnlyFans platform.

They're undoubtedly shrewd enough to understand the industries that she's involved in must be more than tangentially aligned with the Adult Video News program they've just learned she's about host, but the whole *parent's daughter thing* is making it near-impossible to illuminate entirely.

Jessica is doing her best to bridge the gap, again with the subtlety of a rabid raccoon in a dumpster fire as she frenetically describes the depths of their daughter's influence on the 'alternative entertainment' community.

Bob/Dad and Helen/Mom feign interest in the specifics of her various jobs and do not feign interest in the specifics of her earnings, switching subjects only after learning specifics of the family member they're about to acquire.

(Well, Helen/Mom does—Bob/Dad bounces in and out of the conversation regarding Marcus to discuss his rock-solid investment strategies—until her private equity firm/hedge fund enlightening quietly assures him that she's much better money than he ever was.)

She's admittedly more nervous about this dinner, and how it will turn out than the AVN's and how they will turn out; mercifully and *un*, Marcus didn't give her much warning, having arranged their flight out here and subsequent stay without her knowledge/consent and before last week's surprise engagement.

Halfway through dinner, she's begrudgingly acknowledging that it's better this way, more time to focus on next week's awards ceremony and the various pressures associated with the Episode 1 release and less time to contemplate scolding associated with the whole *leaving her hometown and on short/no notice* thing.

Miraculously that scolding doesn't come, dinner ending hours later and with Helen/Mom and Jessica crying over stories of their shared 'special little girl' and Bob/Dad politely and figuratively measuring dick size with Marcus, telling stories the way she assumes all men do.

They leave the restaurant after calling what will be *their* parents an Uber and ensuring they'll give them a proper tour of the city on the weekend; she pretends she doesn't hear Helen/Mom's wine-influenced suggestion that they extend their stay and attend the awards, closing the door *literally* on her Uber and *figuratively* on the idea she's harbored of their resentment for her because she left—the reality/reminder of their love a welcome end to a whirlwind week, latest in a life full *of.*

CHAPTER TWENTY NINE

AVN

thoughts for Thots.

She's on stage, and she's nervous and for a good reason.

She's hosting the motherfucking AVN awards, having walked/hopefully not stumbled across a gigantic stage in gigantic heels, the lights from overhead reflecting off of the sequins on her ridiculously expensive/small sequin dress and making *this,* the moment she's to read the introduction on the teleprompter that's too fucking far away, easily the most difficult thing she's done in her whole life.

Most difficult, only since she bought a ticket for that bus, she reminds herself—and that turned out okay too—and so she parts her perfectly-plumped lips and

kills the monologue

and because, really, killing it is something she just kind of does.

In the front row, she can see Marcus beaming, even-more-than-his-usual projection of support and positivity, looking particularly dapper in his tuxedo and deservedly attracting the attentions of the significant and not-so-significant porn personalities surrounding him. She makes a note to point him out later, going over the next series of monologues in her mind as she finishes the first, deftly introducing the presenters of the first award before moving out of the spotlight and exhaling tremendously, giving herself a significant mental pat-on-the-back.

Doing her best to relax and enjoy the moment, she scans the crowd for familiar faces, reflecting on the year that was and has culminated here and now, slightly-off-center-stage at the event representing the pinnacle in an industry she fell into.

Some seven rows back, she spots Jessica—spots her and only because she's standing and waving frenetically, drawing not only her attention (as intended) but the momentary attention of the presenter on stage—the presenter who momentarily stumbles introducing the nominees for the first award, Big Bust Production.

Beside Jessica, Helen/Mom and Bob/Dad are appropriately horrified, having extended their stay and—thanks, as always, to Marcus and his connections—managed to snag significantly excellent late-notice tickets.

While she's sure that she held their rapt attention during the opening ceremony, the combination of the just-awarded category name, and the ones to follow

Best Anal Production

Best Anal Sex Scene

Best Anal Series

Non-Binary Performer of the Year

MILF Performer of the Year

have their heads turning and faces red, looking mortified and seated amongst a sea of barely-clothed/beautiful exhibitionists. She winces visibly, surprising herself at her ability to feel and for them, shifting her gaze instantly and to focus on anyone/thing other than the uncomfortable presence that is *their* presence.

Hollywood Rick is here, some sixteen rows back and staring, looking remarkably less beautiful than she remembers and hopefully for the beating he sustained at the hands of her now-fiancée and that 12-inch dildo.

On the complete opposite end of the auditorium, Tomas and Frederick are crying and blowing her kisses and waving almost as enthusiastically as a still-standing Jessica.

Grateful for the combined support, she returns to the task at hand, introducing presenters for awards like

Best Comedy (really!)

Best Cinematography

Best Director-Drama

Best Foreign Director

and coming to appreciate and *fully* the industry she's showcasing. Seeing the emotions of the award recipients and the pride of the nominees at their collective inclusion, she's discovering an enthusiasm for the porn industry she couldn't have imagined growing up in some small town back home.

She's wondering if some young girl (hopefully not *too* young) is watching this show on the internet and dreaming of being on the stage she's standing on the way she used to as a little girl watching the Academy Awards, that bus ticket at least partly influenced by presentations not-too-far-removed from this one.

She's watching the next series of awards presented from the best seat in the house when a reaction from Jessica in the crowd focuses all of her attention on the here and now.

Favorite Cam Girl

nominees have just been introduced by two beautiful-but-unfamiliar presenters; they've just announced that the winner of the award has recently retired from the business, something about having secured a deal with FashionNova.

She's unfamiliar with the brand—other than recognizing that seemingly every mid-to-upper tier Influencer has a deal as a FashionNova ambassador on Instagram—and, when the winner's name is announced to a sea of applause, no one applauds louder or more viscerally than Jessica.

So as the former cam girl formerly known as

Staycee Kiss

takes the stage and the award for

Favorite Cam Girl

she's equally astonished by her beauty and by Jessica's wailings; wailings, she notes, that are more enthusiastic than the wailings she's been wailing for *her*.

She's mesmerized as the former cam girl formerly known as Staycee Kiss makes her impassioned acceptance speech, admiring her beauty and her body and her tattoos and her grace and her comfortability on stage as she regales the audience with a monologue far more impressive than anything she could hope to deliver.

She has the crowd roaring, stories of her unfortunate OnlyFans handle *ThotFineAss420* and of unfortunate encounters with fans—by the time she thanks her best friend Jessica and for *everything,* she can't help but wonder what *everything* is and why Jessica, balling in the audience and blowing kisses back, has never mentioned someone so clearly *not* unmentionable.

Staycee Kiss ends her astonishingly impressive acceptance speech by thanking

The Mother Fucker Who Caused All This

and, as she exits stage left, she can't help but feel sorry for the dirtbag loser who left a goddess like *that*.

. . .

Hollywood Rick wins the next award,

Best Male Performer

and he wins it over Rod Hardson, bringing a sobering/infuriating damper on what has otherwise been an amazing evening. Apparently, the footage of his behaving like a buffoon/receiving a significant beating, captured in the effectively titled

Porn Stars Gone Wild Episode 1: The Emasculation of Hollywood Rick

only added to his mystique; that trending on Twitter and being the topic of porn-related podcasts for weeks post-debacle have earned him significant clout.

He accepts the award with the patented sleaze she expects of him; her applause is fake and forced, and for the camera as she moves to introduce the presenters for one of the final awards of the evening, ignoring the wink he winks at her and half-praying he twists his ankle on the stairs as he leaves the stage.

She introduces the presenters for

Best New Starlet

aware that she's one of the fifteen nominees and for the film that Hollywood Rick just took home

Best Male Performer

for. Marcus and Tomas and Frederick assured her that—
while her performance was sufficiently amazing—the
emergence of a far-more-hardcore/potentially morally
ambiguous/gender-fluid star named Candy Gapes is
likely to overshadow her; *Pornstars Gone Wild*
remembered more for the chaos *on* set than the
performance captured *in* it.

She's entirely fine with this, somewhat eager to be
finished with this amazing evening and somewhat eager
to be finished with this amazingly restrictive series of
one-for-each-segment dresses; she's picturing the after-
party and a much-needed glass of champagne, and she's
picturing a relatively fast exit, home and a waiting bath
on her mind when

Monica Starr

her stage name is called,

Monica Starr

called because—in addition to hosting—she just won the
award for

Best New Starlet

at the motherfucking AVN's.

BOOK THREE

You + Her.

thoughts for Thots.

CHAPTER ONE

& Only.

thoughts for Thots.

You're sitting across the trendy Hollywood restaurant table from

her

and you kind of feel it's like looking into a mirror.

It's not, because you're

Staycee Kiss

and she's

Monica Starr

but you're cataloging a series of admittedly impressive similarities.

Chief among them is a friendship with Jessica, who arranged this meeting and is holding court from the chair to your left, filling any potentially awkward empty space with hurried one-way conversation.

So Jessica is, for lack of a better term, cataloging your various accomplishments and cataloging her various accomplishments in lieu of a forced and semi-awkward introduction, and you're looking at

Monica Starr

(Sarah)

and here at this trendy Hollywood restaurant and for tonight only, you're the way you haven't been in a long, long time. You take a moment to acknowledge that no one has really called you by your real name (Jessica notwithstanding) since Esteban/Steve, and so when she uses it before discussing your acceptance speech at last week's AVNs, you're forgiven for taking a second to recognize that she's not gushing over someone else.

She's beautiful, beautiful in the way Influencers of her ilk sometimes-always are, her hair as black as the black tablecloth her wine glass rests-and-never-for-very-long-on, her eyes the kind of odd color that warrants the investigating you're continually doing. You admire her lack of augmentation, her lips naturally pouty and her cheeks appropriately full, a rarity in the city they've come to call home and have since—as Jessica continues to recount—conquered.

Even their occasionally-interrupting waiter has had work done, making your respect for Sarah's spot in the porn hierarchy sans fake tits/ass/lips/all-ribs-intact even more impressive than Jessica is right now making it sound.

She finishes, Jessica, some half-a-drink later, finally leaving enough air in the room for you to converse. You do, back and forth for the next two hours, sharing stories of respective ascensions and sharing best practices and—as it turns out—sharing ideas for mutually beneficial and financially lucrative collaborations.

...

She can't get over how beautiful this woman is.

She's sitting across a trendy Hollywood table from her, and she kind of feels it's like looking into a mirror.

It's not, because the woman across the table is

Staycee Kiss

and she's

Monica Starr,

but the similarities are remarkable.

In station and prestige and accomplishment, as Jessica— seated to her right and running them down one-by-one notes; she's more interested in analyzing the elements of her breathtaking beauty. The augmentations she not-alarmingly/obviously has are somehow subtle enough to compliment her features, a rarity in a town living by Jessica's

more is more

philosophy. Even the waiter's work is more obvious, her perfectly pumped-up perfect little lips just one cc shy of fake looking. Her cheekbones are high and just enough, not distracting from the honey-colored almond-shaped eyes Michelle is looking *through* her with. The freckles likely tattooed just under them are as well done as the tattoos adorning her arms—she leans forward with a warm smile and an exaggerated bend at the waist powerful enough to break eye contact and have her admiring the perfectness of her undoubtedly expensive breasts. Her loose, honey-colored hair (thick and extended by undoubtedly equally-expensive extensions), falls over them, threatening to hide her view. This only goes on for a moment, as she--unconsciously aware of a need to keep them always in view—runs her fingers through her hair and (with an overly suggestive arch of her back) removes any hint of obscurity.

She's perfect, and so the proposal she came here to propose—the proposal created with Jessica and designed to take advantage of her Producer clout in the *Nu-*Hollywood porn space—is proposed without that extra glass of wine she thought she would need to propose it.

Finding the courage, she parts her perfectly-plump non-filler filled lips and asks

How would you feel about a collaboration

hoping that the proposal that follows heralds a return to the industry she knows no one really gets away from.

Given the amount of money they stand to make, why the hell would anyone want to?

These, she muses, looking into her big, beautiful, make-a-ton-of-money-off-of-them-eyes, are Thoughts for Thots.